SHAMELESS
Kimberly Raye

HARLEQUIN®

TORONTO • NEW YORK • LONDON
AMSTERDAM • PARIS • SYDNEY • HAMBURG
STOCKHOLM • ATHENS • TOKYO • MILAN • MADRID
PRAGUE • WARSAW • BUDAPEST • AUCKLAND

For my mother,
for always being there.
You're the best!

ISBN 0-373-25891-7

SHAMELESS

Copyright © 2000 by Kimberly Raye Rangel.

This edition published by arrangement with Harlequin Books S.A.

® and TM are trademarks of the publisher. Trademarks indicated with ® are registered in the United States Patent and Trademark Office, the Canadian Trade Marks Office and in other countries.

Visit us at www.eHarlequin.com

Printed in U.S.A.

"By the way—" Nell's voice followed him "—you've got company waitin'."

"Company? Who—" The back door slammed and Jimmy had no choice but to find out who his guest was for himself. He popped the tab on his beer and headed for the partially open study door. It was nearly ten at night, and the sidewalks in town rolled up at five. *Who in the world—*

She was sitting on his desk, her long legs stretched out, her three-inch red stilettos tapping an impatient tempo.

Jimmy smiled as his gaze shifted, skimming up slim calves, shapely knees and thighs that disappeared beneath the edge of her black leather coat. *A coat? In July?*

Green eyes met piercing blue as Deb Strickland got to her feet, her hands going to the belt that held the edges of her coat together. Jimmy's grin faltered.

"So, are we going to do this, or what?" Deb asked in a husky voice.

Before he could reply, the edges of the coat fell open and Jimmy got an up close and personal view of the woman who'd haunted his nights for the past year.

Only this time, the woman was real. And she was here, she was naked and she was *his*.

For the next two weeks, anyhow.

Dear Reader,

Writing books for the Blaze miniseries is like a dream come true for me. I love hot, intense stories that aren't afraid to push boundaries and explore the sensuality buried deep down inside all of us. I'm thrilled to be back this month, and next, bringing you two steamy reads that feature the wickedly handsome Mission brothers.

For those of you who read my first Blaze novel, *Breathless*, you might recognize bold, passionate Texas bad boy, Jimmy Mission. He's back, and he's hot on the trail of city gal, Deb Strickland. Jimmy and Deb are the least compatible people in Inspiration, Texas. The trouble is, they can't seem to keep their hands off each other. When they decide an affair will sate their mutual lust, the result is nothing short of *shameless*....

Next month, get set for another Texas bad boy. When Jack Mission returns home to Inspiration, he promptly turns prim and proper Paige Cassidy's life upside down. Divorced from a man who swore she could do nothing right, Paige is on a major self-improvement kick. And sexy, *restless* drifter Jack Mission is just the man to give her lessons in love. Look for *Restless* in August 2000.

For those of you who wrote asking for Deb and Jimmy's story, I hope you enjoy *Shameless*. I truly appreciate your encouragement and excitement!

Happy reading,

Kimberly Raye

P.S. I'd love to hear from you! You can write to me c/o Harlequin Books, 225 Duncan Mill Road, Don Mills, Ontario, Canada M3B 3K9, or visit me on-line at www.kimberlyromance.com.

_____ Prologue _____

HE TASTED as good as he looked.

Warm. Wicked. *Hungry.*

Firm lips flavored with a hint of raspberry—as if he'd just had a drink at the nearby refreshment table—ate at hers, nibbling, coaxing, taking their own sweet time despite the swarm of carnival goers and the line of men, dollar bills in hand, who waited behind this tall, delicious cowboy for a kiss of their own.

Yes, there were more men to kiss, more dollars to be had. Inspiration's only elementary school needed new books for the library. A worthwhile cause, and the main reason Deb Strickland, owner and editor of the small Texas town's only newspaper, had agreed to man the kissing booth in the first place. That and the fact that she had a bad reputation to uphold, even if it was all fiction and little fact. No healthy, single, red-blooded, dare-anything city gal would turn down the chance to play lip lock with the town cuties.

Cute being the operative word. As in nice, friendly, like the widower Mitchell from the feed store who gave her a stick of gum every time she stopped by, or Marty from the diner who gave her extra French fries on her lunch plate, or Paul from the gas station who blushed every time she looked at him. "Filler" men in the big newspaper of life.

This guy qualified as a lead story.

He'd looked the typical cowboy with his straw Resistol, faded denim shirt and jeans and dusty brown boots. But there'd been nothing typical about his bright green eyes, as vivid as a stretch of rich pasture on a summer day, or his full sensuous lips that had curved into a teasing grin just as he'd stepped up to her in the booth. He was blond and beautiful and hot. Definitely hot.

She wondered briefly why she hadn't seen him around before. She'd been living in Inspiration for over six years now and she made it her business to know every handsome man within a fifty-mile radius—a self-proclaimed wild woman always knew the available pool of men even if she didn't get her feet wet.

She was drowning now, she realized, lost in a wave of heat and passion and *him*. He sought a deeper connection, and Deb did something she hadn't done since she'd taken her place in the booth. She opened her mouth and kissed back.

His tongue stroked and teased hers and everything faded. The *whirrr* of the cotton candy machine, the *ding* of the Shoot-n-Hoop, the whine of a Tammy Wynette record blasting at the cakewalk next door.

Her thoughts centered on the mouth melding with hers, the strong hand cupping the back of her neck, the callused thumb stroking the curve of her jaw, the five o'clock shadow that rasped her tender skin.

Mmm.... The tantalizing scent of leather and sawdust and sexy male filled her nostrils and kicked up her heartbeat. Her nipples sprang to life, pressing hungrily against the lace of her bra, wanting...just *wanting*. Heat pooled low in her belly, spreading, licking at the insides of her thighs the way his tongue licked at her mouth.

Her body hummed and heat sped along her nerve endings until she burned and ached, and at nothing more than his kiss. His touch. *Him.*

"Hurry it up!"

"We ain't got all day!"

"Give another fella a chance!"

She wasn't sure how much time had passed when the voices finally pushed past the pounding of her heart and tugged her back to reality, to the smell of popcorn and the cry of a fiddle and the all-important fact that her hands were gripping the table edge, her knees were trembling and her lips were locked with a total stranger's, and all in front of an impatient audience.

Not a stranger, a small voice whispered, a sense of familiarity creeping through her. As if she'd known him before.

Crazy.

She was crazy. And her hormones were desperate. For all the men in town who'd claimed to have scored with "Daring Deb," few had ever made it past first base. It had been a long time since Deb had felt a man's touch.

Too long, she thought as she pulled away and concentrated on gathering her composure, which wasn't nearly as easy as it should have been. Not with him so close, his green eyes fixed on her, mirroring her own disbelief, as if he also was stunned by the past few seconds.

Say something, her brain screamed.

I really liked that.

Can we do it again?

And again?

And more?

"Here," was all she managed as she handed back the dollar bill he'd given her.

He glanced at the money. "What's this for?"

"I should be the one paying you."

He grinned and the sight was almost as heartstopping as his kiss. "I think the kids need it more than I do." He placed the dollar into her palm and curled her fingers around it, his skin brushing hers, setting off a wave of tingles that shimmered through her and made her nipples throb. "Speaking of kids." He glanced at his watch, a frown sweeping away his dimples. "I'm due at the dunking booth right about now."

"You're a volunteer?"

He nodded. "Maury Hatfield suckered me into sitting in his oversize fish tank for an hour."

"At least you'll be getting wet for a good cause," she managed, her lips still vibrating from his kiss. She blew out a deep breath and wiped a trickle of sweat from her temple.

"Hot?" His eyes twinkled and she knew he wasn't just talking about the weather. More like lips touching and tongues dancing and her body responding....

"You can't even imagine."

His strong fingertip caught the slow glide of perspiration down her neck and slid up, over the curve of her jaw. "Oh, I think I can." His thumb swept her still trembling bottom lip. "Damn straight I can." His voice grew huskier, deeper, meant for her ears alone. "Meet me at the dunking booth when you're done here, Slick, and we'll see what we can do about cooling off." Then he gave her a slow, lazy wink and disappeared into the crowd.

Slick. The word registered in her head, pulling and

tugging at a long ago memory, of a shy, quiet four-teen-year-old who'd come to spend yet another sum-mer vacation with her granny.

Deb had treasured those times with her granny Lily. The few precious days when she'd been able to eat and sleep and breathe without asking permission. To smile and pretend that all was right with the world, that her last name wasn't Strickland and her future wasn't already mapped out for her.

She hadn't known it at the time, but that fourteenth summer would be her last in Inspiration for a while, and her most memorable. Particularly one hot July day when she'd been in town shopping. Granny had gone into Shelly's Boutique while Deb had lingered outside the Mr. Freeze, struggling with the strap of one of her new sandals, a low-heeled, hot pink num-ber she'd bought behind her ultraconservative fa-ther's back.

"Hey, Slick. You just gonna stand there, or you gonna put those fancy shoes to good use and come on in?"

Her head had snapped up. Her fingers faltered on the leather strap as her gaze collided with a pair of deep, green eyes. The owner, maybe seventeen or eighteen, was the stuff teenage fantasies were made of with his crooked smile and tall, athletic body. He held the door open for her. Music and laughter drifted from inside the ice-cream shop, enticing her as much as the boy's smile. Almost.

But Deb had lived with her father's rules much too long to be seduced that easily. She managed to shake her head.

"That's a shame." He grinned. "Maybe next time."

And then it had happened. Her first wink from a real boy, and not just any boy. *The* boy.

"Jimmy Mission," she murmured as her pounding heart came to a shuddering halt.

Deb had moved to Inspiration six years ago to discover Jimmy, town golden boy and star running back for the local high school, had joined the marines right after graduation. Other than the occasional brief visit to his folks, he'd never looked back. Thankfully, because at that time Deb hadn't needed the added complication of facing the one and only man who made her feel like that shy, insecure fourteen-year-old she'd been so long ago.

But that girl was history. She'd buried her insecurities, her past. Now she was bold and brassy Deb Strickland. Independent. In control. Completely immune to men like Jimmy Mission with their easygoing, cowboy charm.

Or so she'd told herself when she'd heard he'd come home a few months back, just days after his father had passed away. Since then he'd been running the ranch, caring for his grief-stricken mother, and, rumor had it, looking for a wife.

Deb fought down a wave of disappointment. Of all the men to kiss her pantyhose off, it had to be hardworking, family-oriented, marriage-minded *him*. Was there no justice in the world?

"Pucker up, missy." An old man with a handlebar mustache shoved a dollar at her and leaned forward.

"Sorry, Cecil. We're closed."

"Since when?"

"Since I've got a date at the dunking booth." Deb fished into her pocket, pulled out a few twenties so the kids didn't miss out on the money from the kisses she was about to decline, stuffed the cash into the till and flipped on the Out To Lunch sign. A quick adjustment of her blazing red jacket and silk blouse, and she rounded the table and headed through the crowd of people.

When she reached her destination, her heart stalled at the sight of him, clad only in jeans, sitting up on the raised platform. Blond hair sprinkled his chest and funneled to a thin line that bisected a rippled abdomen. The tanned muscles of his arms flexed, bulged as he gripped the edge of his seat and dangled his bare, tanned feet in the water.

The girl at the head of the line tossed the ball and missed, her gaze hooked on him rather than the bright red target just to the left. Deb could sympathize. He was buff and beautiful, with a wicked smile and brilliant eyes and...

The thought died as his gaze caught hers and she felt an answering warmth deep inside. His lips curved, a dimple cut into his right cheek, and the warmth turned to full-blown heat.

Deb, heart racing, hormones chanting, body wanting, did the only thing she could. She traded her money for a stash of balls, aimed for the target and let the first ball rip.

Marriage-minded Jimmy Mission had husband written all over him and the last thing, the very *last* thing Deb Strickland wanted was a husband. She'd come too close to making that mistake once before.

Never again.

No matter how good he kissed.

1

One year later

JIMMY MISSION wasn't sure what bothered him most
about Deb Strickland.

The fact that she was pleading her innocence to the
judge, even though the entire lunch rush at Pancake
World had seen her back into the front end of his
Bronco.

Or the fact that with every deep breath she took,
her low-cut silk blouse shifted and a heart-shaped tattoo played a wicked game of peek-a-boo with him.

"*Four thousand dollars? For a little dent? Why, with
a hammer and five bucks worth of spray paint, I
could fix the blasted thing myself!*"

"Six hundred is for the dent." Skeeter Baines, the
oldest judge in Inspiration and an ex-fishing buddy
of Jimmy's late father, pointed a bony finger at her.
"The rest is for poor Jimmy's pain and suffering.
Maybe you'll think twice before you go ramming that
fancy sports car of yours into an innocent man's
truck."

"Innocent? Judge, it was his bumper that was sticking over the line into *my* spot. I couldn't help but tap
him."

"Three times?" the judge asked.

"It was twice."

"Aha! So you *did* ram him."

"*Tapped* him, and my insurance will cover the damages. As for the pain and suffering—"

"I've made my decision. Now take your seat." The judge slammed his hammer down and Deb blew out an exasperated sigh.

The tattoo flashed Jimmy in full, heart-shaped splendor—a vivid red against a backdrop of pale, satin-looking skin—and his mouth went dry.

"This is a terrible miscarriage of justice," she declared, pivoting to face the handful of people clustered in the tiny courtroom—the bailiff, the court reporter, the police officer who'd responded to the accident call and three nosy file clerks. "Grossly unfair." Another deep sigh, a quick flash of red, and Jimmy's groin tightened.

The only thing unfair was Jimmy's reaction to the brunette stomping around the defendant's table in three-inch heels, a tight red skirt and a clingy white blouse.

This was Deb Strickland, he reminded himself. Ten percent soft, warm, female, ninety percent ballsy attitude, and the woman responsible for causing him so much grief. He rued the day he'd had the misfortune to lay down good money for an all-too-brief kiss that had started out their renewed acquaintance with such sweet promise. After she'd dunked and damned near drowned him that same fateful day, things between them had only gone downhill.

"What is unfair, Miss Strickland," Judge Baines snapped, "is that you purposely damaged Mr. Mission's property."

"Desperate times call for desperate measures.

Jimmy Mission has been hounding me for an entire year. Every time I turn around, there he is."

"This is a small town, Miss Strickland."

"I'm fully aware of that, but he's not only *there*, he's doing things—like parking in my spot every time he comes into town, sitting in *my* seat at *my* table during the YMCA charity barbecue last month, signing up to be *my* partner during the wheelbarrow race at the Senior Citizen Olympics."

"Attended that barbecue, myself. Sounds like Jimmy was just being charitable and looking out for his own, which is more than I can say for present company."

"This is about Cletus Wallaby, isn't it?" When the judge's expression hardened, Deb added, "You can't hold that against me, Judge. Cletus Wallaby was a crooked councilman and the people of this town deserved to know it. It was my journalistic duty to expose him."

"Cletus was born and raised here. Spent his whole life struggling to make the town better when you were just a gleam in your rich father's eye."

"Homegrown or not, he stole money from taxpayers and that makes him crooked."

"He may have fudged on his expense sheets for the town, but he's a damn good family man and a helluva fisherman, little missy, and you'd do well to remember that some folks don't take too kindly to outsiders spreading rumors."

"Every one of my facts was documented and proven. That's why he was fired last year. *Fact*, not rumor."

"And the *fact* here," the judge snapped, obviously

set in his opinion despite the proof, "is that you damaged Jimmy's property."

"But he was taking up half my space—"

"Try two inches," Jimmy called out, adding fuel to the already out-of-control fire that blazed between them. "I was barely two inches beyond the line, Judge."

She turned blazing blue eyes on him and what he'd discovered to be her most intimidating glare.

Only Jimmy wasn't easily intimidated or put off. He could handle women, even an ornery one.

He gave her the slowest, laziest grin he could manage with just a hint of a wink, an expression he'd become notorious for since he'd first used it to con Mary Sue Grimes into the bed of his daddy's pickup when he'd been fifteen. Jimmy didn't really understand the effect of "The Grin" on women, just that it never failed to turn the tide his way.

She glared. "Two inches is about the size of things, from what I hear."

"Now, Slick." His grin widened when her gaze narrowed. "I didn't think you listened to hearsay. If you want to check your facts, I'd be mighty happy to show you and set the record straight."

"I just bet you would," she snapped.

Deb Strickland didn't, wouldn't respond to "The Grin." Aside from the moment they'd kissed, she hadn't responded in any positive way to him since he'd come home to Inspiration over a year ago and found her running the town newspaper in place of her granny Lily.

He'd been surprised. Not because Deb had taken the old woman's place at the *In Touch*, but because she'd grown from the scrawny young city gal who used to keep her granny company a few weeks every summer into one fine-looking woman who, folks said, kept company with every eligible man in town.

Every man, that is, except for him.

It puzzled the hell out of Jimmy, not only because of her initial response to him, but because women, all women, just plain liked him. It was a fact of life, like the sun rising and setting, his mother baking her famous Christmas cookies, his Black Angus bull walking away with first prize at the Austin County livestock show. Jimmy smiled and women smiled back. He flirted and they flirted back.

And some did more, he thought, eyeing the platter of petit fours sitting in front of him, courtesy of the court reporter, Justine something or other, and Daring Deb's Fun Girl Fact for the week—*Go get 'im with gourmet goodies!* He thought about the drawer full of silk underwear—not his own—he had at home due to last week's *Seduce him with silk!* He pictured his cabinet overflowing with everything from biscotti to croissants, smoked oysters to sardines, all surefire aphrodisiacs according to *Loosen him up with love potions!*

He glanced down at the folded newspaper and today's words of wisdom. *Nothing says come and get me like pineapple-flavored body glaze!*

This was a small Texas town. Most of the women hadn't even heard of flavored body glazes, much less seen a tube of the stuff, which was exactly the point of the column. To bring some city-savvy love advice to the single women of Inspiration.

Jimmy had nothing against women being savvy when it came to love, he just didn't want all that savvy directed at him when he wasn't ready to do anything about it. Most of the women he knew wouldn't get all spruced up for a man unless he'd already handed over the ring, and Jimmy hadn't even narrowed down the candidates, much less decided on the future Lady Mission.

He knew Deb had started the column to push him away, to draw the line between them and remind him that she wasn't the sort of girl a guy could take home to his mama. But damned if she didn't come back every few weeks with some short, serious article. Like the one she'd done on Cletus Wallaby who'd cost the good citizens of Inspiration major tax dollars because of his falsified expense reports, or the one she'd done to rally support for the local animal shelter.

It was those serious, caring articles that never failed to cool his anger and stir his admiration. And they also made him wonder exactly how many rumours regarding Deb's bedroom exploits were rooted in fact and how many were pure speculation based on the sophisticated, worldly image she portrayed and the fact that this was a small town and gossip a favorite pastime. He knew she'd dated all of the twenty or so eligible men in town. What he had trouble swallowing was that she'd bedded all of them, because as turned on as she'd been by his kiss, he'd sensed her surprise, as well.

"Don't you have better things to do than harass innocent women?" Deb's voice drew Jimmy back to the here and now and the fire flashing in her blue eyes.

"Sure do. Today, I'm teaching a lesson to a guilty woman. You break the law, you have to pay."

"But you parked in my spot on purpose."

"Barely." He shrugged. "I'm not too good at parallel parking."

"Well, neither am I. So sue me." The minute the words were out of her mouth, a wave of red crept up her neck and fueled her cheeks.

"That's what I'm doing, sweetheart."

And in a big way. He'd counted on the fact that Judge Baines, still soured over Deb's exposure of Cletus, the judge's longtime fishing buddy, would go for the maximum judgement allowed. Having his early weekend fishing trip put off by a Friday morning hearing didn't help matters. Deb didn't stand a chance, which was exactly why Jimmy had hauled her into court.

Not that he needed the outrageous judgment. This wasn't about damages. It was about finishing what they'd started.

She wanted him. He'd felt it, seen it, even if she had spent the past year denying it. He'd no more been able to forget the taste of her—warm woman and sweet peppermint and sinful promise—than he'd been able to shake the urge to breathe. Over the past year, reading her articles, seeing her around town, talking to her, hell, even arguing with her, had intensified the attraction. She was in his head, under his skin, in his blood.

At first, he'd tried to deny the chemistry between them. He'd been so damned mad after the dunking booth incident, which had been her intention all along. To push him away, piss him off, keep distance between them. She wanted him, but she didn't want to want him because she, like every other female in town, knew he had marriage on his mind. If there was one thing he'd learned about Deb Strickland, it was that she was single and proud of it.

Good. While Jimmy did have marriage on his

mind, he wanted a strong, solid woman who knew
her cattle better than her cosmetics. One who wasn't
afraid to get her hands dirty to give one hundred percent to a thriving ranch that demanded so much.

Too much.

He shook away the thought. The ranch was his life
now, and he would do what he had to do. For his
mother and father. For the future of the Mission
spread. Duty called, and so he didn't, *couldn't* want a
woman like Deb Strickland, with her fancy clothes
and painted nails and city-slicker persona, in his life.

But in his bed, wearing nothing but a smile and
some pineapple-flavored body glaze...now that was
a different matter altogether.

Deb huffed, the heart flashed, and Jimmy's body
gave an answering throb.

"I'm begging you to rethink this, Judge Baines."

"No time, missy. I've got a great big catfish with
my name on it out in Morgan's Pond and you've
made me as late as I'm gonna get." The gavel
slammed down as the judge stood up. "I rule in favor
of the plaintiff for four thousand dollars." He
shrugged off his robe to reveal a plaid shirt and blue
jeans, and grabbed the rod and reel propped in the far
corner. "Good day and happy fishing."

Jimmy barely had time to stand before the three file
clerks and the court reporter closed in on him.

"Congratulations, Jimmy."

"You deserve it."

"How'd you like that sardine sandwich I made you
last week?"

By the time Jimmy smiled and talked his way past
the women, Deb Strickland and her tattoo had disappeared.

He should have been thankful.

She was sure to come at him, guns blazing, ready to rip his head off and mount it on the wall above her desk over at the *In Touch.* He'd waited this long to make his proposition. A few more days, maybe even a couple of weeks wouldn't make much difference. Besides, Jimmy had always been a patient man where women were concerned, which was why he'd invested so much time in pursuing a woman with such a hands-off attitude.

He had work waiting—a plowed over fence in the north pasture, a pen full of cattle needing vaccinations, and Valentino, his stud bull, was due in Austin tomorrow to be photographed for a layout in *Texas Cattleman* featuring prize livestock.

He needed to get things settled, to pack. He didn't need a confrontation to take up more time when he was already running short.

But damned if he didn't want one.

DEB FOUGHT to keep from shedding even one of the tears burning her eyes as she headed down the hallway. Deb Strickland didn't cry, no matter how grossly unfair Judge Baines's verdict.

Four thousand dollars. Where was she supposed to come up with that kind of money?

With barely two thousand left in her own savings account—a quarter of which she'd already planned to transfer to the newspaper account to help cover Wally's salary—she was scraping bottom already. She had three hundred open on her Visa, eighty bucks in her checking account, Granny Lily's decrepit house, a car that wasn't even halfway paid off, a lifetime supply of Go Girl cosmetics she'd won back in a magazine competition in college and a newspaper that barely generated enough revenue to cover expenses.

Most of the time, it didn't, which was why she'd nearly depleted the nest egg Granny Lily had left her.

She fought back the urge to turn around, stomp back into the courtroom and punch the plaintiff's infuriatingly handsome face.

She would have done in a second except she'd traded Sonia at the beauty shop a month of free advertising for a French manicure just yesterday. She wasn't about to waste a precious nail on some pig-headed cowboy, even if said cowboy was Jimmy Mission.

Especially because it was him. He was completely off-limits. Cowboy non grata. The more distance between them, the better.

"Hey, Slick, wait up." His deep voice rumbled behind.

"Get lost." She picked up the pace.

"I want to talk to you."

"And I want to strangle you, but lucky for you my personal beauty regime prohibits physical violence. Go away."

He stopped, but his voice followed her. "Why are you so dead set on running away from me?"

The question rang in her ears, prickling her ego and she turned on him before she could think better of it. "Why are you so dead set on ruining my life?"

"Last time I looked, *you* hit *me.*"

"You parked in my spot intentionally. You've been doing it for months just to tick me off." Eleven months and fifteen days to be exact, since their first and last kiss, not that Deb was counting....

Oh, God, she *was* counting.

She glared at him. "You've been hogging my spot on purpose."

"And you've been avoiding me on purpose, that or trying to piss me off."

She managed a laugh but could hardly feel mirthful since, even though a few feet separated them, the scent of him reached her. The enticing aroma of leather and male and that unnameable something that made her think of satin sheets and champagne and... Forget it. Forget him. Forget the kiss. *Forget.*

She tried for a steadying breath. "Look, I realize you're very popular, but unlike the other members of your fan club," she motioned to the group of women clustered outside the courtroom, their gazes hooked on Jimmy. "I'm too busy to spend my valuable time thinking about ways to piss you off."

"Really?"

"Really."

"You know what I think?"

"I couldn't care less."

"I think," he said, stepping toward her, "you've been pushing me away on purpose, hoping I'd back off because you're scared."

"Scared? Of what? You? The day I'm scared of you, buster, is the day Myrna Jenkins—" known to the entire town as queen of the coiffure "—goes to the Piggly Wiggly with her hair in rollers."

"Not me, Slick." He took another step, closing the distance between them. "*Us.*" The word trembled in the air between them.

She craned her neck and stared up at him. "There is no *us.*"

"We were good together."

"For about five seconds."

"It was more like ten." His gaze narrowed. "But a kiss is just a kiss, right? A little fun?"

He'd obviously read her article, just as she'd intended. She'd written the piece right after she'd finished up at the carnival and gone home to an empty house, disappointed and frustrated because Mr. Kiss-of-the-Century had turned out to be Mr. Jimmy Mission. Inspiration's most eligible husband prospect was completely off-limits to a woman like Deb who'd sworn off marriage and family when she'd left Dallas. So she'd written one of her most powerful editorials, entitled Girls Just Wanna Have Fun, which had led to her weekly and ever-popular Daring Deb's Fun Girl Fact.

"Not every woman's out to find herself a husband," she told him.

"And not every man's out to find himself a wife."

"But you are."

"Says who?"

"Everyone in this desperately small town." She eyed him. "So what's the scoop? Are you or are you not looking for a wife?"

"Not at this moment."

"What's that supposed to mean?"

"That, yes, I'm keeping my eye out for the future Lady Mission. I'm thirty-two and it's time to settle down, but until I find her—and your column hasn't made things any easier by turning half the women around here into pushy—"

"Assertive," she cut in. "Fun women are assertive."

"And convinced that being a good wife means rubbing herself down with pineapple-flavored body glaze and doubling as a Christmas ham."

Despite the heat and the tension, a grin tugged at her lips. "Actually, a *very* good wife rubs herself down with pineapple glaze and doubles as a Christmas ham."

"That's where you're wrong, honey. A very good wife doesn't waste her time on foolishness. She steers a tractor, rides fence and pitches hay right alongside her husband. But that's neither here nor there. I'm talking about something a lot more basic. If a girl can have her fun, so can a guy."

She peeked around him and eyed the women still gathered in the hallway. "I say take your pick and go for it."

He grabbed her arm and hauled her toward the alcove behind a nearby stairwell.

"What are you doing—" she started, the words drowning in the lump in her throat as he whirled her around and cornered her.

"I pick you."

She stared up at him, wishing he wasn't so tall, so handsome, so...close. "I'm not ripe for picking."

His eyes darkened and she realized she'd said the wrong things...or the right thing depending on the part of her doing the thinking. From the heat pooling between her thighs she'd lay down money it wasn't her head.

"I'd say you're definitely ripe, honey." His thumb grazed the nipple pressing against her blouse and heat speared her. "Damn near ready to burst."

"That's not what I meant." She summoned her most nonchalant voice. "You should really save your energy for a nice girl who's into the tractor thing."

"The whole point is to expend a little energy."

"So do it with the future Mrs. Jimmy Mission."

"I would, but I haven't found her yet."

"Then expend energy with one of your fans out in the hallway."

"I've known each one of them nearly all my life, and while they're having a good time reading your articles and playing at being savvy singles, they're really only after one thing—a husband. The morning after, I'm sure to find an anxious father waiting on my doorstep with a loaded shotgun, and Preacher Marley standing next to him. I'll end up hitched whether I've found the right woman or not."

"What makes you think the same won't happen with me?"

"You got an anxious father waiting at home?"

Once upon a time... She shook away the thought and fought back a wave of guilt. "No."

"You know Preacher Marley?"

"He's an *In Touch* subscriber."

"How likely is he to step in and defend your honor?"

She stiffened and met his stare. "For your information, I can defend my own honor."

"There was never a doubt in my mind." He touched her then, skin to skin, the tip of one finger at her collarbone, and heat bolted through her from the contact. "You're something when you get all stirred up." He traced a path lower, until his fingertip came to rest atop the tattoo peeking from the vee of her blouse. "This drove me crazy all morning."

Before she could form a reply, he dipped his head and the tip of his tongue flicked over the sensitive area. A moan caught in her throat and she closed her eyes, the pleasure sweet, intense, overwhelming.

"You've been driving me crazy all year," he went on. Sexy green eyes caught and held hers. "You've been haunting my dreams. You and your red lips and that damned kiss and this heat between us."

Amen. While Deb had heard about chemistry and animal attraction and how, sometimes, things just sparked between two people, she'd never felt it. Sure, she'd been attracted to men, but the pull had never felt so...desperate. Like if she didn't have him, she'd die. Right here. Right now.

"Don't you think it's about time we stopped all this nonsense?" he asked.

Boy, did she ever. She caught the words before they could pass her lips and drew her mouth into a tight line. "You want to talk about nonsense? That judgment. My insurance will cover the damages, but anything above and beyond is ridiculous."

"And still your responsibility."

"But you weren't anywhere near that Bronco when I tapped you. Why should I pay you pain and suffering?"

"I've been in pain since the first moment I tasted you—" his fingertip skimmed her bottom lip "—and suffering every night since because I want to taste you again." His gaze flicked to her mouth. "The law is the law. You owe me, Slick."

"I don't have four thousand dollars."

"I don't want four thousand dollars."

Don't ask. Turn. Walk away. Do anything but ask.

Something about the intense light of his gaze compelled her, however, almost as much as the need that suddenly gripped her body.

"What *do* you want?"

"This, for starters." And then he kissed her.

Jimmy Mission tasted even better than she remembered. Hotter. More potent.

His hand cupped her cheek, the other splayed along her rib cage just inches shy of her right breast, his fingers searing through the fabric of her blouse. His mouth nibbled at hers. His tongue slid wet and wicked along her bottom lip before dipping inside to stroke and tease and take her breath away.

Now this...*this* was the reason she'd dunked him at the carnival.

Because she'd been a heartbeat shy of crawling into the dunk tank with him, throwing herself into his arms and begging for another kiss. No way could she have allowed herself to do such a thing with a marriage-minded man like Jimmy Mission.

A girl had to have her standards, and married men, engaged men, men who walked and talked and reeked of home and hearth and tradition, like Jimmy, were completely off-limits. No marriage for her. Just freedom and fun and...

The thought faded as his fingers crept an inch higher, closer to her aching nipple which bolted to attention, eager for a touch, a stroke, something... *anything*.

His fingers stopped inches shy, but his mouth kept moving, his tongue stroking, lips eating, hungry...so hungry. His intent was pure sin, and Deb couldn't help herself; a moan vibrated up her throat.

He caught the sound, deepening the kiss for a delicious moment that made her stomach jump and her thighs quiver, and left no doubt as to the power of the chemistry between them.

She'd been burning for him all these months, the flames fed by memories and fantasies and his constant pursuit.

"What are you doing to me?" she murmured, dazed and trembling, when he finally pulled away.

He leaned in, his breath warm against her ear. "Not even half of what I want to do." His words made her shake and quiver all the more.

Shaking? Quivering? Over a man?

This man, a voice whispered, that same voice that had warned her off him so many months ago. The voice that kept her one step ahead of him because no way was Deb Strickland going to find herself trapped all over again. She was free now, and she was staying that way.

She pulled away, desperate to put some distance between them and find the common sense that seemed to desert her every time he was near. "I've got work to do."

"Don't even think about running now," he cut in, his fingers tightening on her arm, his hold firm but not painful. His mouth grazed hers before she could tell him exactly where to get off. "I'm calling your bluff, Slick." The words vibrated against her lips. "You say all you want's a little fun. Well, that's all I want. You. Me. Two weeks of fun. No strings attached. Then we'll call it even." He gave her another lingering kiss before letting go of her. "Think about it."

2

"SO WHAT DO YOU THINK?"

"That's the dress?" Deb asked as she stared at the wedding gown Annie Divine, her best friend and star reporter—make that ex-reporter—had just pulled from a large white box.

"There has to be some mistake." Annie's frantic fingers rifled through the layers of tissue paper and white satin. "This isn't the dress I ordered. Laverne!" she shouted past the drapes that hung over the dressing room doorway of Inspiration's only bridal shop. "They sent the wrong dress!"

"They couldn't have." Laverne Dolby, proprietor of the dress store and president of the local Reba McIntyre fan club, shoved the curtains aside. "I've been here nigh on twenty-five years and not once..." Her words faded as she pulled heart-shaped, rose-tinted glasses from her pile of Reba-red curls, and slid her second pair of eyes into place. "Land sakes, this is the dress my niece, Rita Ann, ordered."

Hope lit Annie's tear-streaked features. "So if I have hers, she has mine, right?"

"'Fraid not. Hers—I mean, yours is on back order. Won't be in for another six weeks."

"But my wedding's in exactly three weeks. What am I going to do?" Annie turned stricken eyes on Deb.

Deb handed Annie a tissue and turned to Laverne. "We need another wedding gown."

Laverne shook her head. "All of mine are special order. I've got a nice selection of bridesmaid dresses, some mother-of-the-bride, that sort of thing. As for wedding dresses..." Her gaze fell to the box. "Hey, I bet Rita Ann wouldn't mind you wearing this one. Her wedding's not for two months. I could let you have this one and get her another."

Another glance at the dress and Annie burst into fresh tears.

"I guess this isn't exactly what you had in mind," Laverne said. "Lordy, this is a pickle."

"A *pickle?*" Annie cried. "This is the worst day of my life! And here I thought I was finally going to have a happily ever after with Tack." Annie Divine and Tack Brandon had been high school sweethearts. Tack had been the captain of the football team, handsome and popular, and Annie had been invisible. Somehow, and Deb felt certain it was because Annie was as sweet and understanding as Texas was big, she and Tack had gotten together. They'd been right in the middle of a hot high school romance when Tack's mom had died in a tragic accident. He'd left the Big B, a large ranch bordering the Mission spread, and spent the next ten years racing the motorcross circuit. Finally, he'd come home for good and set his sights on Annie who'd been working for the *In Touch*, aspiring to be a big-time reporter.

Annie had tried to resist him, but her love, still alive after all these years, had won in the end. She'd decided she'd be happier freelancing for magazines and making babies than working for a major newspaper.

While Deb wasn't too keen on the baby part—her own mother had passed away when she was three and she'd never really experienced the nurturing-mother phenomenon up close, much less developed a craving for it—she still wished Annie every bit of happiness.

"I should have known something would go wrong." Annie's words faded into a series of sniffles and choked sobs.

Sympathy tears burned Deb's eyes and she blinked frantically. "Laverne," she snapped, dashing away one lone, traitorous tear before anyone could see, "why don't you go dig up some bridesmaid dresses for me while I talk to Annie in private?" Before the woman could respond, Deb hustled her toward the doorway, yanked the curtains closed behind her. She turned to Annie.

"I'm sorry," Annie blurted. "I'm not usually such a mess." She wiped at her face. "It's just that I've still got to find a photographer and a florist, pick out and mail the invitations and find a caterer and a baker. And Tack's racing friends are coming in next Saturday. I don't have time to drive to Austin and look for another dress."

"We'll figure something out." Deb studied the gown. "You know, this material's not half bad."

"How can you tell with all that stuff on it...?" Annie's words faded as her gaze locked with Deb's. "I know what you're thinking and you can just forget it. This dress is awful."

"That's because it's just lying there. Formals always look that way. Then you put them on, and *voilà*, it makes all the difference in the world."

A moment of thoughtful silence passed, punctuated by a huge sniffle. "You think?" Deb nodded and Annie seemed to gather her courage. "You know, you're probably right. I'll just try it on and maybe it won't be so bad." Minutes later, she turned her gaze to the surrounding mirrors and burst into another bout of tears. "Forget it. It's horrible."

"It isn't horrible. It's just…different." Deb searched for the right words as she stared at the rows of beaded roses, the miles of tulle, the myriad of white silk ribbons and appliqués of all shapes and sizes. "Busy."

"It's worse than downtown Houston during rush hour."

"True, but we can fix it. We'll cut here, rearrange there, take off the bows and the overabundance of sequins and beadwork and it'll be perfect."

"Laverne can handle hems, but this is major—"

"I'll do it."

"You?"

Deb fingered the lapel of her champagne-colored suit. "Who do you think made this?"

"I was thinking Saks or Gucci."

"Way out here in Timbuktu, Texas?"

"They have catalogues. And you do drive to Austin every now and then. I thought maybe you did some power shopping."

As if she had the cash for that. "Granny Lily taught me everything she knew and left me her sewing machine to keep me company."

Annie eyed the gown. "You really think you can do something with this?"

"Girlfriend, I know I can." Deb wiped at Annie's smudged cheeks with a tissue. "Now cheer up and let's get on with this fitting."

Annie sniffled and looked hopeful as she glanced into the mirror. Her expression fell as she surveyed her reflection. "Forget it. This is white."

"What's wrong with white?"

She gave Deb an "Are you kidding?" look.

"Oh, please, Annie. If you think everyone who wears white in this day and age is as pure as the driven snow, guess again."

"It's not that. It's just…Tack and I have been living together the past few weeks and—"

"If anyone deserves to wear white, it's you," Deb cut in. "It's your first wedding with your first and only true love. I don't care how long you've been living together or what wicked things you do in the privacy of your own bedroom."

Annie grinned. "Or the barn."

Deb arched an eyebrow. "The barn?"

"Then there was that time down by the river."

"The river?"

"And on the back of Tack's motorcycle."

"A motorcycle?" Deb shook her head. "Goody-goody Annie Divine has done it on the back of a motorcycle, and I can't even find a decent date. What's wrong with this picture?"

"You tell me." Annie peeled off the dress and handed it over to Deb. "You used to be out every night dusting the floor down at BJ's with some hunky cowboy. Lately, the only vehicle reported after hours at your house belongs to the pizza delivery boy."

"A girl's gotta eat." Deb avoided Annie's curious gaze and inspected the dress. She'd get rid of the cupids and the extravagant beading.

"You're not mopey because of my wedding, are you?"

"Believe me, it's not that." She would do away with the godawful bows.

"Because your turn will come one day."

"I don't want a turn." The sequined butterflies were history.

"And you'll be standing here in a big white dress of your own."

"I hate white." *Adios* beaded tulips.

"And you'll walk down the aisle with the man of your dreams."

"The man of my dreams avoids aisles." The rhinestone ladybug buttons didn't stand a chance.

"And you'll both say 'I do' and it'll be happily ever after and—"

"It's *not* the wedding," Deb cut in. "It's..." She shook her head. "I've just had a lot on my mind lately." An understatement if she'd ever made one.

Think about it. It had been a full month since Jimmy Mission had murmured those words. During that time, she'd seen him only once, the evening following their day in court. She and Annie had been having drinks at BJ's and he'd walked in. After a few heated glances and the usual bickering, she'd walked out. Actually, *run* was a more appropriate verb.

She'd been so sure he meant to get his answer then and there, and she hadn't been up to giving him one. She'd been too angry and much too aroused after their second kiss to think clearly. But he'd kept his distance because Jimmy Mission had obviously meant what he'd said.

He wanted her to think.

To simmer.

"Is some man causing you trouble?" Annie's voice drew Deb's attention and she shook her head.

"*Definitely* not." Jimmy Mission wasn't causing trouble, he *was* trouble. He was too good-looking, too charming and she wanted him entirely too much.

She didn't need to get involved with a man who had his sights set on marriage. Marriage led to family and family to sacrifice and sacrifice to misery. She knew because she'd spent the better part of her life sacrificing her own happiness for the sake of family, and being miserable because of it.

But, and this was the biggie, Jimmy didn't have marriage on his mind; he wanted an affair. In a sense, he was offering to leave four thousand dollars on her nightstand, payment for services rendered.

The thought should have made her feel cheap. She should have exploded with righteous indignation at the suggestion, promptly refusing and made good on the judgment by offering him free advertising for his stud bull or a partnership in the paper. That's what the proper, conservative daughter of newspaper mogul Arthur Strickland would have done.

But Deb had traded propriety for freedom a long time ago. She wanted her debt, however ridiculous, paid in full and quickly. Jimmy's offer not only promised that, but much, much more.

"Deb?" Annie's voice intruded on her thoughts and she shook away images of the *more*. Namely, Jimmy kissing her again and again and...

"Are you listening?"

"Hmmm?"

"There is something wrong."

"No, there isn't."

"I just mentioned the word pastel and you didn't react."

"Pastel what?"

"Dresses."

"Bridesmaid dresses, right?"

"There are no bridesmaids, just a maid of honor—you." When Deb only nodded, Annie frowned. "Now I know something's wrong."

"Because I agreed to wear pastel for my best friend's wedding?"

"Because you—Miss I'm-a-winter-complexion-and-I-only-wear-bold-colors—agreed to do it without any grumbling."

"I'm grumbling." Deb tapped her chest. "In here, where it counts."

Annie eyed her. "You aren't worried about the nominations, are you? Why, you're a shoo-in."

"I'm not a shoo-in, and it doesn't matter."

"Of course it matters. Being nominated by the Texas Associated Press for Best Weekly newspaper is a huge honor, and after the year you've had and the headline articles you've done, you're sure to garner a nomination. You'll probably even win, so you'd better line up a formal and get ready for a major awards ceremony."

"I don't want a nomination." *Liar.* "And I'm not going to any stuffy awards ceremony." The last thing Deb wanted was to run into her father after she'd managed to avoid him for so long.

Another speculative glance and Annie asked, "Then you're not still worried about that court judgment, are you?"

Damn but Annie had a sixth sense when it came to spotting trouble. "Hardly."

"Because I know the *In Touch* isn't making you rich."

"I didn't buy it to get rich." No, she'd bought it to

hold on to a piece of Lily. Sweet, caring Lily, who'd given her the best memories of an otherwise lonely childhood. Lily, who'd taught her to sew and encouraged her fashion design aspirations when her father had done little more than frown and bark "No" when she'd asked to go to design school. Lily, who'd always understood and never passed judgment.

Every time Deb walked into the tiny newspaper office, she could still smell the woman's perfume. A mixture of vanilla and jasmine that sent a wave of peace through her. Lily had loved the *In Touch*, and Deb had loved Lily, and buying the paper, going there day after day, felt right.

"You know, I'm sure Tack would be willing to loan you the money."

"I don't borrow from friends." From anyone. Deb Strickland paid her own way in life. That way her freedom was never compromised.

"Then talk to Jimmy. I'm sure you two can come to an agreement."

"I will. Now stop worrying about me and let's see about finding a maid of honor's dress."

They spent the next half hour cruising the racks in Laverne's until Deb had accumulated an armload of possibilities. Annie went to the rear of the store to look at gloves, while Deb headed back to the dressing room.

She shed her jacket, shimmied out of her skirt and peeled off her silk blouse, then reached for a floor-length pink slip dress.

"Annie," she called out through the open curtain as she fumbled to undo a row of tiny pearl buttons. "Come and see what you think about this." She con-

tinued to struggle with the fastenings, silently curs-
ing their impracticality.

"I think it looks great." A deep, familiar voice slid
into her ears and sent a prickle of heat to every erog-
enous zone—from her earlobes to her nipples, the
backs of her knees to the arch of each foot, and many,
many spots in between.

Her hands stalled and she became keenly aware of
three important facts. Number one, she was almost
naked. Number two, she was almost naked in front of
Jimmy Mission who lounged in the dressing room
doorway. Number three, she was almost naked in
front of Jimmy Mission, *and* it made her very nervous.

Nervous? Since when did she get nervous in front
of men?

She pushed aside the sensation and concentrated
on the buttons rather than the handsome picture he
made standing there wearing jeans and a denim shirt,
the sleeves rolled up to the elbows.

"Better than great," he added. "That's definitely
my favorite dress."

"But I'm not wearing it yet."

A fierce green gaze swept the length of her in a leisurely motion that made her nipples pebble and press
against the cups of her favorite Swedish lace bra.
"That's the point, Slick."

"Do you mind? I'd like a little privacy."

He grinned and stepped inside the room. The curtain swished shut behind him.

"That's not exactly what I meant." She put her back
to him, as if that could shut him out. The room, set up
like a giant octagon, had mirrors on all sides and she
couldn't escape his reflection. "If I didn't know better, I'd say you were trying to rattle me on purpose."

His gaze captured hers in one of the mirrors. "But you know better, right?"

For a split second, she was fourteen years old again, staring into his green eyes as he held the door open, that damnable smile on his face as he waited.

That's what he seemed to be doing now. Waiting. Watching.

She shook away the notion. She was a good fifteen years away from that painfully shy and sheltered girl, and she'd faced down men even better looking than Jimmy Mission.

Even so, her lips trembled around the next words. "What are you doing here?"

"Getting fitted for my tux. In case you've forgotten, I'm Tack's best man."

"I meant *here*. In the dressing room. *My* dressing room."

"I saw Annie and she told me you were in here. I thought it was high time we talked."

"I'd definitely say a month constituted high time."

Green eyes twinkled. "If I didn't know better, I'd say you were mad."

It was her turn to toss his words back at him. "But you know better, right?" He grinned and an echoing shiver went through her body. She turned to the dress and struggled with the buttons.

Before she could take her next breath, he stepped up behind her, his arms came around and his hands closed over hers. "I wanted you to have plenty of time to think," he murmured as long, lean fingers helped her work the buttons through the openings.

She tried for a calm voice. "Of a way out?"

"A way in, Slick." His deep, compelling voice vibrated against the shell of her ear. "It's much better that way."

"You're not very funny."

His hands fell away and he let her slide the last button free, but he didn't step back. He simply stood there, behind her, close but not touching. "I'm deadly serious."

That was the trouble.

Trouble? Since when? He was a good-looking, virile man, and while she didn't make it a habit of bedding everyone who fell into that category—despite her reputation to the contrary—she wasn't exactly a virgin. She was attracted to him, and he'd conveniently wiped away the one barrier that had kept her from acting on her feelings. *No strings attached.*

"What if I say no?"

"I turn and walk away. We'll work something out as far as the money goes and our business will be finished."

He was giving her a way out.

One she would have taken in a heartbeat, except that their unfinished business had nothing to do with her debt and everything to do with the heat swamping her senses.

Since their first kiss, he'd become a part of her life. Jimmy Mission, with his wicked smile and his hungry lips, had become the star of her most erotic fantasies, the hero of her romantic dreams, the image that stole through her mind whenever another man smiled or flirted or merely tipped his hat.

One taste of him had led to a dangerous addiction that she desperately needed to kick, and sleeping with him would surely satisfy the curiosity his kisses had stirred. Surely. Then she could get on with her life, with running her newspaper and living each day on her own terms. No one dictating her every action, her every thought. No one stealing through her mind and working her hormones into a frenzy.

"I've been thinking about you, Slick." His fingertip prowled along the slope of her bare shoulder and goose bumps danced down her arms. Her fingers went limp and the dress slithered to the carpeted floor.

She managed to swallow. "Oh, yeah?"

"Yeah." He closed the heartbeat of space between them, his denim-covered thighs pressing against the backs of her legs, his groin nestled against her bottom so she could feel just how much he had been thinking about her. His cotton shirt cushioned her shoulder blades. The material brushed against the sensitive backs of her arms as he slid his hands around her waist. Strong, work-roughened fingertips skimmed her rib cage, stopping just shy of her lace-covered breasts.

It was highly erotic watching him in the mirror, his dark hands on her skin, his powerful body framing hers. It was even more erotic seeing her own response to him—the rosy flush creeping up her neck, the goose bumps chasing up and down her arms, the part to her lips, the plump of her breasts as her breath caught. It was almost as if she watched someone else, yet more intense because it wasn't someone else. It was her. Him. *Them.*

"So pretty," he murmured huskily as warm hands cupped her breasts.

"You like Swedish lace?"

"I was talking about this." He fingered the tip of one dark nipple peeking through the scalloped pattern. "And this." He touched the other throbbing crest, rolled it between his thumb and forefinger. "Definitely the prettiest thing I've seen in a long time."

Heat speared her and she barely caught the moan that slid up her throat.

"You like this, Slick?"

"I..." Her answer faded in the swish of drapes. Jimmy's hands fell away a heartbeat before Laverne's familiar voice echoed around them.

"I found a couple more dresses you might like—" The words stumbled to a halt as the woman came up short in the doorway. Her gaze ping-ponged between Jimmy and Deb, and she frowned before a thought seemed to strike. "You two doing research?"

"Research?" Deb managed.

"For that there column of yours. You and Jimmy working on the next Fun Fact—"

"We *are not* doing research."

"Not yet," Jimmy murmured, his voice for her ears only. Then he turned a smile, bright enough to melt Iceland, on the shop owner. "I got lost."

"Lost? In here?"

"Sure enough. You've expanded the place since I got fitted for my last tux. You remember that?"

A smile chased the suspicion from Laverne's expression. "Your high school prom. You and Tack Brandon liked to turn my hair gray making me comb half the state looking for neon purple cummerbunds. You were every bit as sassy back then as you are now."

"And you were every bit as pretty. Harold's a lucky man."

Laverne blushed a shade bright enough to match

her dyed hair. "That's what I keep telling him, but he listens about as well as he washes dishes."

Deb would have laughed at how easy the woman was taken in by a little masculine charm, except that her own heart was still pounding ninety to nothing.

"Anyhow," Jimmy went on, "I was trying to find my way to the men's dressing room when I heard Deb, here. She needed help with her dress, and I've never been one to resist a damsel in distress."

"The, um, buttons stuck," Deb added. Oh, God. Was that her trembling voice? No way. Her voice didn't tremble, not on account of some man.

She stiffened and snatched up the forgotten pink dress. "Come to think of it," she snapped, "this thing has way too many buttons. Do you have anything with a zipper?"

Laverne glanced at the pile in her arms and fished a dress free. "Try this." She handed over a buttercup yellow shift with a side zipper before turning to Jimmy. "You come on with me, sugar, and I'll give you a personal escort back to the men's dressing room."

"I'd be mighty obliged."

"By the way," Laverne asked as she hooked her arm through Jimmy's. "Did I ever introduce you to my niece, Lurline? Why, she's the prettiest girl in the county and she knows her chicken feed from her horse grain, let me tell you. You two would hit it off perfectly and I just happened to mention that you were getting fitted today. She's right outside...."

"We'll settle this later," he told Deb as the shop owner led him from the room.

Later, as in he was giving Deb more time to think. To worry.

To fantasize. And now after their too close encounter a few moments ago, she had even more fuel for those fantasies.

Forget it.

"Yes," she blurted and he stopped, the motion jerking Laverne back a step.

His gaze caught hers. "Yes to what?"

"The two weeks." She took a deep breath and tried to slow the blood zinging through her veins. "I'll do it."

His grin was slow and heartstopping. "You mean, *we'll* do it." Then he winked, and did the last thing Deb expected.

He walked away.

3

HE'D WALKED AWAY.

That all-important fact replayed in Deb's head later that day as she sat at her desk at the *In Touch*, the three-room newspaper office located right above Pancake World.

But he hadn't walked. He'd sauntered, swayed, in that long-legged, sexy-as-hell gait that made an entire bridal shop full of women—most of them Laverne's single cousins and nieces and even her great aunt who'd just *happened* to stop by—drop their jaws and visibly salivate.

And not just on account of his looks. Sure, Jimmy had it all put together right, but it was the entire package that made him the hottest catch in four counties. He was the green-eyed, blond-haired, handsome white knight every girl dreamed of. The charming, honest, loyal son-in-law mamas prayed for. The successful, salt-of-the-earth rancher every daddy wanted to see hitched to his little girl.

It was strictly Darwin's theory at work. Society looked to the strongest, most appealing for procreating. While the dreaded *P* word was the last thing Deb had in mind, she wasn't immune to Jimmy's appeal.

In fact, his appeal had had her *this* close to wrapping her arms around him and begging for more of what he'd started with his warm hands and purposeful fingers.

By walking away, he'd dashed that impulse.

"Why are you frowning?" Wally, Deb's devoted copyboy, had glanced up from his computer and was eyeing her.

"I'm not frowning." She busied herself taking a sip of black coffee from the latest acquisition of her collection of designer Bitch mugs: I've Got The Itch To Bitch.

"You're definitely frowning. Isn't she frowning?" he asked the seventy-something woman who sat at a nearby table.

Dolores Guiness had eyes and ears as big as Texas, which was exactly why Deb had hired her on for a few hours a day to write the About Town section, aka the gossip column for the *In Touch*. The old woman made it her business to know everything about everyone.

She eyed Deb over a pair of black-rimmed bifocals as if she were a coyote sizing up a good rib eye. "Why *are* you frowning, dear? You can tell old Dolores."

"I'm not frowning."

"You sure are," Wally persisted. "Isn't she?" This time he turned to the petite redhead who sat at what had once been Annie's desk. She wore an oversize white T-shirt that swallowed her small frame and a pair of blue-jean overalls.

"I, um, I guess so."

"It's okay to speak your mind," Wally said. "She won't bite you."

"I definitely bite," Deb told the timid Paige.

"Rumor has it she definitely has biting potential,"

Dolores informed them. "But since said biter signs my paycheck, I'm keeping my opinion to myself."

"Good girl," Deb told her.

"She likes everybody to think she bites," Wally went on, "but she doesn't."

"I bite, dammit." Deb took another sip, slammed her mug down on her desk and glared at Wally. "And don't you go telling anybody otherwise."

"I don't have to tell anyone anything. You already did it yourself when you led the fundraiser for those foster kids over at the church. And when you organized that bake sale to help Mr. and Mrs. Cootie pay funeral expenses for their uncle. Stuff like that speaks for itself. You're definitely a nonbiter."

"I'm the editor of the town newspaper. I like to stay in the thick of things. My reasons are purely self-motivated."

"And we're expecting a blizzard to blow through central Texas tomorrow. She's like one of those Eskimo pies," he told Paige. "Hard shell, soft filling."

Deb glared. "Don't you have work to do?"

"That depends."

She pasted on her most intimidating frown. "On whether or not I'm firing you for insubordination?"

"On whether or not you really meant it when you said I could take over Annie's duties."

"Of course I meant it. You get Annie's job. Paige gets your job. Dolores gets to dish dirt part-time."

"Okay—" he rubbed his hands together "—if I'm now officially a full-fledged reporter, photographer—"

"—part-time printing press mechanic," Deb cut in. At his frown, she added, "You know that old press better than anyone."

"I hate that old press," he grumbled, "but I'm willing to continue sweating blood over it if you'll let me handle the This Is Your Neighbor interview this week."

"That's my column."

"I know. I'll just be filling in for you the way Annie used to."

"She only did it twice when I happened to be over-booked. I'm not overbooked. I've already got the in-terview set up for tomorrow. Mary Jo's going to do it poolside so she can show off the lifetime supply of western swimsuits she won when they crowned her Rodeo Queen. Do you know they actually sent her a thong bikini made out of rawhide leather? It's got a fringe and a great big tassle right over the..." Her words faded as she noticed the gleam in Wally's eyes. "I doubt she'll wear the thong during the interview."

He sighed. "A guy can hope."

"Actually, based on how easy it was for Milton Kelch's boy to get her to the Inspiration Inn last Sat-urday night, I think it wouldn't take much for her to wear the thong," Dolores said, her old grey eyes twinkling, "or nothing at all."

Deb let Wally sweat for a full minute as she sipped more coffee. "I'll tell you what," she finally said. "If you can finish reinking the press before you leave, you can have the interview."

"Hot damn!" He winked at Paige. "I told you, an Eskimo pie."

When the young woman looked at her, Deb meant to give her best frown. She had a reputation to main-tain, but the look in the frail-looking redhead's eyes struck a deep chord. Uncertainty. Loneliness. Fear.

Once upon a time six years ago, Deb had known all three.

She smiled, Paige's expression eased, and a quiet settled over the office, disrupted only by the steady click of computer keys and the chug of the window unit pumping ice-cold air through the large room.

It proved to be an unusually calm Friday, more so because Deb found herself eyeing the phone on several occasions, a strange sense of expectancy in the pit of her stomach.

"Something's definitely wrong," Wally said when he accidentally handed Deb his herbal tea by mistake, and she drank it. "Let me guess, Jasmine couldn't work you in at the beauty parlor and you're having a bad-hair day."

"It's not my hair."

"You used the last of your favorite tube of Vamping Red lipstick."

"I've got half a tube in my purse."

"Your cat ran away."

"Camille is probably curled up on my sofa as we speak." She sighed and fixed her gaze on her computer.

"The Texas Awards. You're nervous we're not going to be nominated for Best Weekly."

"It's not that."

"I told you, it's a done deal."

"I could care less. Just get back to work, would you?"

Wally shrugged and headed back to the printing press, Paige practically disappeared in the pile of advertising copy on her desk, Dolores left for a supper meeting with her head gossip source—the beautician over at the beauty parlor—and Deb did her best to edit her latest piece on the need for a better nursing home facility in Inspiration.

Hours later, after everyone had left, Deb stabbed the button on her computer, flicked off her desk lamp and called it a night.

For the hundredth time, she glanced at the phone. As if she could compel the blasted thing to ring. A glance at her watch and she accepted the inevitable. He wasn't going to call.

It seemed as if Jimmy Mission wasn't all that excited about their deal. She wasn't sure what she'd expected when she'd said yes. At the very least, a few details spelling out the terms of the agreement, such as when and where.

What she hadn't expected was this...waiting. Deb wasn't good at waiting, or wondering or worrying.

Maybe he was just busy. Jimmy was notorious for his commitment to the Mission Ranch. He lived and breathed the place, much the way she lived and breathed the paper.

Or maybe he'd changed his mind. Why give up four thousand dollars when he could have any woman in town for free?

Or maybe he'd been stomped to a bloody pulp by an angry bull—

Her thoughts collided to a stop when she exited the building and saw the young woman sitting on the curb near a worn '57 Impala, tears streaming down her face.

"Paige?"

The young woman's head jerked up and fear flashed in her eyes as she wiped frantically at her face. "Um, hi. I—I was just..." The words faded in a frantic shake of her head. "What difference does it make?" She met Deb's gaze. "You might as well know, I'm a loser. My life sucks, my car used to suck only now it's dead, and I'll completely understand if you want to fire me."

"Fire you?"

She sighed. "Like my last boss. He said, leave your problems at home, Miss Cassidy. I tried, but my problem—my ex-husband, Woodrow—kept showing up at my work, and when Woodrow was upset, he didn't care who heard him. I tried to do everything right. I'd leave his breakfast for him, his clothes laid out, but I didn't cook good enough or iron good enough or do anything good enough." Her shoulders shook with a deep sob. "It's no wonder he left, and it's no wonder this stupid thing died." She kicked the tire. "I can't change the oil and I never learned a thing about fan belts, and I don't know how to fill the radiator with water, and I'll totally understand if you tell me to take a hike. I mean, here I am, sitting in front of the office carrying on and such.... It's shameful."

Deb dug a tissue out of her purse, leaned down and gave the young woman a smile. "Honey, there's no such thing."

Paige took the tissue and cast hopeful eyes on Deb. "You mean, I'm not fired?"

"Do you like working for me?"

"Very much. I loved working on the paper back in high school, which is why I applied in the first place. I love to write and while I'm not actually writing a book or anything—"

"—this is the next best thing," Deb finished for her. Paige nodded and Deb gave her a wink. "You're not fired. That is, unless you don't stop crying right now. Then it's *adios*."

Paige sniffled and wiped frantically at her eyes. "I'm embarrassing you."

"Me? Girlfriend, you are new to town." She indicated the tissue. "Dry up. You're much too pretty to be sitting around moping over some man. Come on. I'll give you a lift home. Tomorrow, we'll have Wally take a look at your Impala."

"That's awful nice, but I couldn't put you out. I live clear on the other side of Mulligan's Creek."

"It's no trouble at all."

"You're really nice, Miss Strickland."

The words sent warmth spurting through Deb. She frowned before the feeling could get the best of her. "It's Deb, and don't mistake kindness for purely self-motivated reasons. I've got a newspaper to run. You're my employee and it's my duty to look out for your welfare."

"Whatever you say, Miss—um, Deb."

They climbed into Deb's fire-engine red Miata and pulled out onto the main strip through town. "So where is Mr. Wonderful now?"

Silence ticked by for several long seconds, as if Paige were trying to work up her courage. "Jail," she finally declared. "He's doing one to two for a dozen counts of check fraud."

"Good. Let's hope they give him some sensitivity training while he's there. That, or a great big horny roommate named Bubba." That drew a smile out of the young woman and Deb patted her hand. "Forget about him. Forget everything he did and everything he said. From what I've seen, you're good at quite a few things. You're a great copy editor, your writing skills are wonderful and you're good at organizing things."

"You think?"

"I've seen firsthand. Not only that, but you're

pretty, too. If this Woodrow wasn't smart enough to realize what a big catch you were, then good riddance. There are plenty of cow patties in the pasture."

"I keep telling myself that."

"Good guys who'll see how beautiful you are. How desirable. How intelligent. Guys who won't make deals with you, then walk away."

"Woodrow and I never made any deal."

"Guys who'll have the courtesy to pick up a phone," Deb went on, her thoughts going to Jimmy, "so you won't sit around wondering whether they're lying in a ditch somewhere."

"Woodrow always called. That was his problem. Everywhere I went, he kept dibs on me. He even called me at the Piggly Wiggly one time. Had me paged."

"Guys who don't walk around with the same damnable grin on their face day after day after day."

"Woodrow never grinned. He scowled a lot, and smirked, but no grins..." Paige's voice faded as she noted Deb's white-knuckled grip on the steering wheel. "Are you all right?"

"Um, yes." Deb relaxed her hands and shrugged. "I was just speaking figuratively, of course."

AFTER DEB dropped off Paige, she headed to her small wood-frame house that sat in the heart of Inspiration, two blocks from the courthouse and town square. The setting sun edged the house in a brilliant orange light, a shadow surrounded by warmth.

Home. That's what this place had always felt like.

For as long as Deb could remember, Lily's had been the only place she'd felt as if she truly belonged.

Certainly not in the monstrous house in River Oaks, an upscale suburb of Houston, where she'd grown up. There'd been a coldness about the twenty-bedroom colonial, while Lily's tiny house held a warmth that seeped clear through to Deb's bones and heated her from the inside out.

Once she'd closed the front door behind her, she greeted Camille, an orange ball of purring fluff, with a soft stroke on the feline's tummy before she slipped off her shoes and shrugged out of her jacket. After she fed the cat, she grabbed a pint of Ben & Jerry's from the freezer, checked the phone to make sure it was on the hook, and sat down on the couch.

A stab of the remote control, and she surfed the limitless cable channels before settling on Country Music Television. While she'd never been a big Alan Jackson fan, if she squinted her eyes just so, the man sort of reminded her of Jimmy.

His image flashed in her head and she closed her eyes, giving herself up to the memory of his reflection in the dressing room mirrors.

His green eyes glittered hot and bright and a tingle of warmth shot through her. Strong, tanned hands spanned her waist, cupped her breasts, plucked her throbbing nipples. The deep timbre of his voice vibrated in her ear.

"You like this, Slick?"

She'd been so close to telling him exactly how much she did like it. How much she wanted more and then—

Laverne.

Her eyes opened and she stared at Camille. "Do you think she actually saw anything?"

The cat purred and Deb shook her head. "It doesn't matter. I'm single, he's single. We weren't hurting anyone. So who cares what she saw?" Not Deb. She did what she liked, with whom she liked, so long as the attraction was mutual, the expectations the same, and the man in question completely unattached.

It was her liberated attitude, rather than her actions, that had earned more than one condemning stare. But Deb had a reporter's intuition, and she knew that while those women were looking down their noses at her, many envied her free spirit, as well.

She knew the feeling. She'd spent a lifetime envying her brothers and the freedom and power bestowed upon them because they'd been blessed with only one X chromosome. Her oldest brother had slept his way through each and every female dorm at the University of Texas. Her father had smiled an indulgent smile, clapped Robert on the back and told him to be careful. Then he'd turned to Deb and told her no, she couldn't go out with a boy because she was only sixteen. Then seventeen. Then eighteen.

No more. She'd given up living with the double standard when she'd left Dallas. Now if she wanted something, she went after it.

As soon as the thought crossed her mind, she became instantly aware of the cold seeping into her fingers. Her gaze dropped to the ice cream carton in her hands, the telephone sitting nearby.

"What the hell am I doing?"

It was Friday night and she was vegetating at home with her favorite comfort food, practically staring at the telephone, waiting for it to ring. Waiting for *him*.

The carton plopped onto the coffee table and the spoon followed as Deb got to her feet. While she might have agreed to his proposition, she'd be damned if she was going to sit around and let him

call all the shots. Deb Strickland didn't wait around
for any man, period. Even if it was Jimmy Mission.

He'd proposed the deal, she'd accepted. It was time
to stop daydreaming and get down to business.

Starting right now.

"Come on, Alice. Don't quit on me. The night's still
young," Jimmy coaxed.

As if the horse knew it was a lie, she tugged against
the lead rope, wanting to lie down, needing to because of the pain.

Jimmy pulled her forward, forcing her to walk, to
keep the pace with him. "It'll be all right, girl," he
soothed. "It always is." The trouble was, the bouts of
colic were getting more frequent, the pain lasting for
longer periods of time. At first, the walking had been
enough, but Jimmy found himself calling Doc Wallaby more often than not.

"Sooner or later you're going to have to face the
fact that she's getting old." Wayne Braxton, Jimmy's
foreman and the best bareback bronc rider in the
county, walked from the barn office a few feet away.

"And?" Jimmy wiped the sweat from his brow and
tipped his hat back.

"She ain't gonna be around forever."

"Maybe not, but she's around now, she's paining,
and I'm walking her."

"You mean I'm walking her." Wayne pulled on his
gloves. "Go sit down 'afore you fall down, boss."

"Look who's talking. You've been up since sunrise."

"True enough, but I haven't been walking a colicky
horse for the past two hours straight, after busting my
ass for the better part of a day. I've had my dinner, a

quick nap, and I'm fired up and spittin' vinegar. Meanwhile, you need food."

"I can eat later."

"And sleep later, I s'pose, and you'll probably tell the Almighty to come back later when he comes knocking because you ain't got time for heaven." Wayne reached for the rope. "You don't have to do every single thing on this ranch by yourself, Jimmy. It's just a horse."

But this wasn't just a horse. Alice had been his first horse, a present for his thirteenth birthday. She'd been one of the best quarterhorses in the county, and he'd loved her the moment he'd seen her at the Austin Livestock Show. Twenty years had slowed her, and while Jimmy had moved on to Emmaline, a younger, stronger horse, Alice was still Alice. His horse. His responsibility. Like everything else.

"Come on, boss. Give it up."

Jimmy hesitated, but finally handed over the rope. "Walk her another half hour. If she hasn't settled down by then, call Doc Wallaby and get him out here to give her a shot for the pain."

"Will do. Now you forget that stack of ledgers in your office and hit the sheets. We got an early day tomorrow."

Jimmy nodded, but both men knew the notion of Jimmy walking back up to the house and straight to bed was about as likely as uncoordinated Curtis Mitchell and his every-which-way-but-loose Palomino winning best showing at the Quarterhorse International.

He gave Alice a last, lingering stroke, made a quick check on Emmaline and the other horses housed in the main barn, then headed up to the ranch house.

The house, a sprawling one-story testimony to the late James Mission's handiwork as a carpenter, sat several feet away, shrouded by towering oak trees. A porch spanned the entire front, the railing made of hand-carved posts that had taken months to craft. But James Mission had willingly put the time into the effort. He'd traded gallons of sweat, more than a few pints of blood and even shed a few tears to build the Mission Ranch from a few acres of pastureland, into one of the most prosperous spreads in the county.

The ranch ain't just a piece of dirt and a few head of cattle. It's who we are, son, who we'll always be.

His father's dream. Jimmy's reality.

He closed his eyes to the throbbing in his temples. He was just tired, overworked.

Frustrated.

The throbbing eased as his thoughts took a turn to the day's events, to the fullest, sweetest, smartest mouth he'd ever had the pleasure of tasting, and the woman who owned it.

I'll do it.

He'd never had a doubt. The chemistry between them was just too powerful to resist. They had only to look at each other, and the air sizzled. He felt it and he knew she did, too. He saw it when her blue eyes turned to liquid cobalt, so hot and mesmerizing his skin felt scorched by a glance. Saw it in the way her chest hitched just enough to swell her breasts and tease him with that damned tattoo.

Even so, he'd still felt an incredible rush of triumph at her words. Anticipation. Excitement. *Want.*

Easy, buddy.

He took a deep breath to slow the sudden rapid drum of his heart. The water trough loomed up ahead and he stopped, cupped his hand and splashed a handful of cool liquid on his face. Another splash, a few deep breaths, and he turned toward the house.

Want or no want, he had a pile of things to do. Receipts to go over. Feed to order. Vaccination charts to check.

While Jimmy had no doubt that Deb Strickland would play havoc with his dreams later on that night, the ranch came first. It always had. It always would.

Jimmy owed his father that much. For teaching him how to ride and rope and giving him the nicest saddle money could buy. For not being upset when his oldest son had traded in that saddle for a bus ticket away from his home and family. While James Mission hadn't understood Jimmy's choice, he'd let him go.

Jimmy fought back a wave of guilt. He was here now and he wasn't going anywhere, and he wasn't looking back. He'd finally smartened up and accepted his destiny. The cattle. The land. The ranch. *Home.*

If only it felt like home.

"Isn't it awful late for you to be here?" he asked when he walked in the back door and saw the sixty-two-year-old woman, silver hair worn in a single braid that reached down her back, leaning over the kitchen sink. She wore a hot pink pantsuit beneath a worn checkered apron that had not only wiped up spills over the past forty years, but a few tears, as well.

Nell Ranger was the same age as his mother and had been the Mission housekeeper all of Jimmy's life. They'd seen each other through first dates—his, way back when, and more recently, her own, since her

husband of thirty-five years had passed on and she'd
started keeping company with Shermin Wilmott, the
seventy-three-year-old square-dance caller over at
the Elks's Lodge.

She shook her dishtowel at him. "If the menfolk in
this family—" which meant Jimmy, since his younger
brother, Jack, barely found the time to call much less
come home for a visit "—would eat like normal people, I wouldn't have to keep dinner waiting to such
an ungodly hour." She indicated a plastic-wrapped
plate sitting on the stove. "I kept the roast hot as long
as I could. You'll have to nuke it if you want it edible."

"I'm so hungry I could eat cardboard." Jimmy
washed his hands and gave Nell a kiss on her rouged
cheek.

She promptly swatted him away and turned to put
the last dish into the dishwasher. "That's about the
taste of it."

Jimmy leaned one hip against the counter, un-
wrapped the plastic, picked up a slice of meat and
took a bite. "Mmmm, best cardboard I've had in a
helluva long time."

Nell closed the dishwasher and tossed her dishtowel at him. "Smartie."

He winked and took another bite before setting the
plate on the counter and wiping his hands on the
towel. "Where's Mama?"

The question sent Nell to the sink, her hands moving a bit quicker as she yanked off her apron. "I'd say
she's probably asleep. Probably be out all night. Yep,
out like a log."

"She that tired?"

Nell didn't say anything, she simply nodded and

Jimmy had the strange feeling something wasn't right.

Of course something wasn't right. His mother had spent the past year pulling away from the ranch. No longer did Jimmy find her out in the barn at sunset or over in the henhouse collecting eggs. She was still mourning, avoiding any and everything that reminded her of her beloved husband. Jimmy even got the feeling at times that she was avoiding him, and it made him all the more determined to set things right.

To be here now when he should have been here then.

"It was our poker night," Nell said, drawing Jimmy from his thoughts.

"So tell me," Jimmy slanted her a grin. "Who got naked? You or mama?"

"I'll have you know, your mama and I are both good, God-fearing Christian women, Jimmy Mission, so get that notion right out of your head, or you can find your own dessert."

That caught his attention. "Dessert?"

"Honey-flavored cookies." She smiled and gestured to the dozen various size jars of honey stacked on the cabinet, all courtesy of last week's Daring Deb Fun Girl Fact, *Sweeten up your honey with honey!* "What else?"

He frowned. "I'll pass."

"You're lucky."

"How's that?"

She handed him the latest edition of the *In Touch*, conveniently folded to this week's Fun Girl Fact: *Nothing says I love you like edible undies!*

He groaned and she chuckled.

"You're evil, Nell Ranger."

"And like I just said, you're lucky. Darned lucky. This is a small town and the nearest pair of edible undies—whatever the hell they are—is at least eighty miles away in Austin. Otherwise, I don't even want to think about what would show up on our doorstep come mornin'." Nell pulled off her apron and hooked it on a peg near the door. "I'm off to see Shermin for a banana split nightcap at the Mr. Freeze."

"So who won the poker game?" he asked as she reached for her purse.

"Your mama, of course."

He groaned again. "Just my luck." The two women gambled with their handmade dolls and Jimmy's mother currently had the bed in three out of eight guest rooms piled with them. For her granddaughters, she kept telling Jimmy—a hint the size of Texas, and one he meant to take to heart when he managed to find the time, not to mention the right woman.

In the meantime...

His gaze snagged on the honey and his thoughts shifted back to Deb, as if they'd ever shifted away. She was always there, lingering in the back of his mind, taunting and teasing and tempting.

Not for much longer. Once he got her into his bed, he'd get her out of his system, and he could concentrate on the ranch and the future again, and forget all about the life he'd left behind back in Houston.

That was at the heart of his attraction to Deb, he knew. She was everything he wouldn't, couldn't let himself have in a woman. Everything he desired. Everything, with her city ways and her free spirit, that he'd given up, and he needed to face that one last time and get the city lust out of his system once and for all.

"I'll be back bright and early for breakfast," the housekeeper said as she opened the door. "Don't stay up too late and make sure you put that plate in the dishwasher."

"Yes, ma'am." He grabbed another hunk of roast, popped it into his mouth and pulled a beer from the fridge before heading down the hallway.

"By the way," Nell's voice followed him, "you've got company waitin'."

"Company? Who—" The back door slammed on his question, and Jimmy had no choice but to turn and find out for himself. He popped the tab on his beer and headed for the partially open study door. It was nearly ten at night. The sidewalks rolled up in town at five, all except for BJ's and the Mr. Freeze. Who in the world....

The thought faded as he walked into the room. His attention snagged on the box sitting on his desk and the bright pink neon words that described the contents: *Scrumptious Strawberry Undies.*

Damn. Someone had actually found a pair.

That same someone was sitting right there, her long legs propped on the edge of his desk, her ankles hooked, three-inch red stillettos tapping an impatient tempo against the desk top.

Jimmy smiled as his gaze shifted, skimming up slim calfs, shapely knees and thighs that disappeared beneath the edge of a black leather coat. A coat? In July?

Green eyes met piercing blue as Deb Strickland got to her feet, her hands going to the belt that held the edges of her coat together. Leather slid against leather and, for the first time where a woman was concerned,

Jimmy's grin faltered. His heart paused and the air lodged in his chest.

"So, are we going to do this or what?" she asked.

Before he could reply, the edges of the coat fell open and Jimmy got an up close and personal view of the woman who'd haunted his nights for the past year.

Only she was real, she was naked, and she was *his*.

For the next two weeks, anyhow.

4

DEB HAD BEEN NAKED in front of her fair share of men, but none had ever made her stomach quiver or her hands tremble the way they were right now.

Of course a *fair share*, in reality, amounted to three and a half, as opposed to the rumored number, which equalled the single male population of Inspiration, plus a few not-so-single males who populated the pick-up section at BJ's Honky Tonk—a back room ripe with receding hairlines, pot bellies and enough testosterone to choke Hercules.

The three included her first love, a pimply-faced football player from a nearby school who'd taken her on her very first date—she'd been eighteen and he'd been nineteen and her father had been livid that she'd defied him for a hamburger and a movie. Then there'd been her steady college boyfriend, a freelance reporter for the college paper. Number three had been the one-night stand she'd had to celebrate the dumping of her fiancé—a man she'd hardly known—and her newfound independence. She'd waltzed into BJ's, and waltzed back out with the first cowboy who'd caught her fancy.

That one night with Jeb Waller, a ranch hand who had since moved on to another town, had set the stage for Deb's scandalous reputation, one she'd fu-eled only once when her bathing-suit top had accidentally popped off during a swim meet at the local junior high school where she'd volunteered as a lifeguard. She'd flashed the head coach—hence the *half* of her three and a half—and set tongues to wagging. Again.

Three and a half. Not a huge number, but enough to yank her out of the running for Miss Virgin Texas. She'd been there and done that, but not once had she ever felt the way she did right now with Jimmy Mission's powerful body filling up the doorway and his hot-as-a-Texas-summer gaze scorching her from her head to her toes and back up again.

He made her feel so excited and anxious and *needy.*

No. She didn't need Jimmy Mission. Her body simply wanted his. *Body* being the operative word.

She forced her thoughts away from her fluttering stomach and shifted her attention to the six feet plus of warm male who hadn't so much as budged an inch since he'd caught sight of her.

At least his feet hadn't budged.

Her gaze lingered on the very prominent bulge beneath his jeans. Her throat went dry and she licked her lips before she could think better of it.

"Come over here and do that, Slick."

Her gaze snapped to his, to the sexy slant of his lips and the knowing light in his eyes, and she was left to wonder if she'd just imagined the flash of raw desire she'd detected when he first entered the room. The same look she'd glimpsed in the bridal shop dressing room. A look that told her she was much more than a convenient way to spend his unchecked lust.

Right. She was as far from Jimmy's ideal as a woman could get, and he was far, far, *far* from hers. He wanted marriage and she didn't.

Of course, he didn't want marriage with *her*. He'd made that perfectly clear.

She stiffened, bit down on her lip, and fought down a strange swell of anger. Anger? More like aggravation. She was standing there naked, for heaven's sake, ready, willing and able, and he was still clear across the room.

"Well?" he drawled.

"Well, what?"

"Why don't you stop giving your bottom lip all that attention and come over here and give me some?"

"Why don't *you* come over here?"

He didn't say a word. Just stared at her with those hot eyes and that ever-widening grin, as if she'd unknowingly delivered the punchline in some private joke of his.

"What are you thinking?" she demanded before she could stop herself.

"That you're about the most stubborn woman I've ever had the misfortune to meet up with."

"I am not stubborn, and for your information, it hasn't been a picnic meeting up with you. You're stubborn yourself, and infuriating and frustrating and irritating—"

"—and you look good enough to pluck from a tree and eat whole."

"—and domineering and... What did you say?"

"You heard me."

She'd heard him all right. His words rang deep and erotic in her ears. *You look good enough to pluck from a tree and eat whole.*

Her gaze shifted to the box and the catch phrase

printed in hot red ink. "But I'm not wearing the undies yet."

Green eyes glittered with a fierce heat that belied the casual smile on his face and made her nipples tingle. "That's the point, Slick."

"Oh." The word barely slid past her lips before he crossed the room in four quick strides.

He stood barely a handspan from her. Filling up her line of vision. Drinking in all her oxygen. Zapping her common sense.

"Oh?" He quirked an eyebrow. "Is that the best the sassiest mouth in the south can come up with?"

Now she was worked up even more, but it had nothing to do with anger over the name he'd called her and everything to do with a bubble of heat that ballooned and popped inside her when he grazed her cheek with his callused fingertip. She cleared her throat and fought for her voice. "The, um, best considering the present circumstances."

"Which are?"

She licked her lips as her gaze riveted on his mouth. He really had a great mouth, with firm, sensual lips that made her skin itch and her insides tighten in anticipation. "It's really hot in here." She blew out a breath and fought for another. "Much too hot to think of snappy comebacks even for a mouth as sassy as mine."

He stared at her long and hard, his grin faltering for a quick second when his gaze dropped to drink in the rapid rise and fall of her chest. "It *is* awful hot to be thinking." He reached out and caught a drop of perspiration as it slid down the valley between her breasts. His touch lingered and her heart thudded a frantic rhythm against his fingertip. "But feeling..."

He stared into her eyes. "I think it's just about hot enough for that. Just—" he angled his head down, his sweet breath fanning her lips "—about."

And then his mouth touched hers.

Deb Strickland had the sassiest mouth Jimmy Mission had ever heard on a woman, all right. And the sweetest he'd ever tasted. Her lips parted at the first moment of contact, and for several heartbeats Jimmy actually forgot that he liked his kisses slow and teasing.

There was nothing slow about the way he stroked his tongue along the length of hers and plunged deep into her mouth. Nothing teasing about the purposeful way he ate at her lips, as if she were his only sustenance and he'd gone far too long without.

He had.

That was the only thought that drew him back to reality and helped him resist the sudden urge to bend her over the desk in that next instant and sink as deep as possible into her soft, warm body, until he forgot where he ended and she began. Until he forgot everything—his ranch and his cattle and his vow to look after both—*everything* save the woman in his arms and the need heating his blood.

Slow and easy.

He gathered his control and fought for a leisurely pace because as much as he wanted Deb Strickland, he wanted to make amends for his past even more. For not being there when his family had needed him most. He couldn't lose his head over a woman all wrong for the life he now lived.

The kiss softened as he suckled her bottom lip and wrung a frustrated moan from her.

He slid his hands up her arms, over her shoulders,

learning her shape, the dips and curves near her collarbone, the soft, satiny slopes of her breasts. He'd wanted her so long, waited so long, and now she was here in his house, his arms, blazing hot at his fingertips.

He lifted her onto the desk, parted her long legs and stepped between her thighs. Her heat cradled the rock-hard erection pulsing beneath his jeans. He thumbed her nipples and caught her cry of pleasure with his mouth, the sound exciting him almost as much as the knowledge that he was finally going to slake the lust that woke him every morning, his body taut and throbbing after a restless night spent dreaming and wanting.

He gave up her lips after a deep, delicious kiss to nibble down her chin, the underside of her jaw. He licked a fiery path to the beat of her pulse, and teased and nibbled at the hollow of her throat until she gasped. Then he moved on, inhaling her sweet, fragrant smell, savoring the flavor of her skin. An echoing flame leapt through him, burning hotter, brighter....

Easy.

He leaned back long enough to drink in the sight of her, her head thrown back, her eyes closed, her breasts arched in silent invitation. Dipping his head, he took a slow, leisurely lap at her nipple. The tip quivered, expanded, reached out and begged for more. He licked her again, slow and easy and thorough, before drawing the pouty flesh deep into his mouth and sucking long and hard. A moan vibrated up her throat and she gasped, grasping at his shoulders.

The grasping he could handle. It was the way she

wrapped her legs around his waist and rubbed herself against his aching length that scattered his common sense. He felt her heat through the tight denim. Anticipated it.

Her desperate fingers worked the button of his jeans, then the zipper. It stuck for a heartpounding moment, the teeth stretched too tight over his straining length. A swift yank, a frenzied *zippp* and he could breathe again.

One silky fingertip touched the swollen head of his erection peeking up at the waistband of his underwear and the air lodged in his throat. So much for breathing.

He caught her head in his hands, his fingers splaying in her hair, anchoring her for the long, deep probe of his tongue.

"Boss!" The slam of a door punctuated the shout, the noise piercing the passionate fog Jimmy found himself lost in. He stiffened, breaking the kiss to gasp for air as footsteps sounded in the hallway.

Deb's forehead furrowed and her eyelids fluttered open. "What's wrong?"

Before Jimmy could answer, Wayne's voice sounded on the other side of the door. "Boss? You in there...?" The words trailed off as the knob twisted, the door creaked.

Jimmy fought for his zipper, but he didn't have enough time. The best he could do in the name of decency was yank his T-shirt down over his open fly as he whirled, Deb's nude body hidden behind him.

"I just got off the phone with Doc Wallaby. Alice rolled on me and—" The words stumbled to a halt as Wayne's gaze hooked on the bare knee peeking past Jimmy's jean-clad thigh. He looked puzzled for an eighth of a second before his ears turned a bright red. "Sorry, boss. I—I didn't know you had company."

Jimmy tried to ignore the soft hands resting against his shoulder blades, the warm breath rushing against the back of his neck. "Is he on his way?"

"Who?" Wayne shook his head as if to clear the cobwebs. "The doc? Yeah. In the meantime, we have to get her up. I figured if anyone could do it, it would be you. But don't worry none, I'll wake up a couple of the hands down in the bunkhouse. With three of us, we should be able to get that stubborn girl back on her feet." Just before the door clicked shut, Wayne said, "You just go back to what you were doing and I'll see to Alice."

The best advice Jimmy had heard in a helluva long time. That's what his throbbing body said, but his conscience, his damned conscience, kept him from turning and taking Deb in his arms.

"Who is Alice?" Her soft question slid into his ears as he fought for a deep, calming breath.

"A horse. My horse."

"Why can't she roll?"

"She's colicky. If she rolls, her insides can get all tangled up."

"Doesn't sound very good."

"It isn't. That's why she has to get up." Why Jimmy had to get her up. She was his horse. His responsibility. *His.*

"Can somebody else help her?" Her cheek rested against his back and he felt her aroused nipples through the thin material of his T-shirt.

He swallowed. "Probably. Maybe. Once the doc gets here, he'll give her a shot and she'll be okay. Right now, she's hurting and that makes her even more ornery." And a hell of a challenge to any man but Jimmy.

He expected a lot of things from Deb, namely the slide of her arms, the touch of her fingertips, a whispered, "Don't worry. It's just a horse." She wasn't a woman to take no for an answer when it came to something she wanted, and she obviously wanted him.

"Then I guess you'd better get to work, cowboy." Her hands slid around his waist and grasped the gaping edges of his jeans. Soft fingertips grazed his erection as she slid the button into place and tugged at his zipper.

His hands closed over hers, helping her until the teeth closed and he was rock-hard and throbbing beneath the denim once again. As if the action had tried her patience as much as his, he heard the deep draw of her breath. Relief.

"You go on," she told him. "I'll see myself out."

Jimmy wasn't about to argue. He started walking, conscious of her eyes on him and even more aware of the need gripping his insides. It would be so easy to turn back to her, to forget about Alice and let Wayne take care of things for the next few minutes while Jimmy sated the lust burning him up from the inside out. Too easy.

He kept walking.

Besides, as eager as he was right now, he wouldn't make it halfway to his bedroom. Deb would be flat on her back on his desk and he'd be inside her in less than a heartbeat, and Jimmy didn't want that. He liked his loving long and slow and fierce. He'd never had much of a fondness for quickies, and he wasn't about to change his ways now on account of a bad case of lust.

Not now. Not ever.

"It's HOT ENOUGH to fry eggs on the pavement," Deb said as she walked into the *In Touch* office the next day, after a night spent tossing and turning and fantasizing, followed by a morning watching the mayor dedicate the brand new public swimming pool just in time for the biggest heat wave to sweep through Texas in twenty years. She plopped her purse and her notebook on her desk.

"I don't know about eggs," Wally said as he pulled a message from a stack on his desk, "But the entire fire department is going over to the parking lot at the Piggly Wiggly at noon with a mess of chickens and some barbecue sauce." At her raised eyebrow, he added, "The fire chief's out to prove that his department needs more funding because the heat wave has them working double time. Meanwhile, the police chief calls him a big whiner and says that it isn't *that* hot and the only department that deserves more funding is the police department. It *is*, too, hot, the fire chief yells back. It ain't, the police chief counters, and so this entire debate starts. The fire chief says it's hot enough to cook an entire chicken in under an hour. The police chief tells him to prove it. Hence, showdown at high noon."

"That's the silliest thing I've ever heard. Anyone can look at a thermostat and *know* it's hot."

"So you don't think we should cover it?"

"Are you kidding? We need a front-page story and seeing Police Chief Miller eat crow should make for a very happy readership."

Red Miller hadn't won his position due to popularity. He was loud and chauvinistic and, worst of all, he'd been caught wearing a Pittsburgh Steelers cap during last year's play-offs with the Cowboys, a fact that had shamed every Mitchell from here to Dallas. Still, he was Mayor Smiley's first cousin, and family was family, especially in Inspiration. People looked out for their own. Their mothers and fathers, brothers and sisters. Their land and cattle and horses.

The last thought conjured an image of Jimmy Mission, that damnable grin on his face as he faced her, his pants unbuttoned and his—

"Here's the copy for the This Is Your Neighbor column." Wally's voice killed the dangerous thought as he tossed some notes onto her desk. "And Dolores said she'll be in later after she's finished getting the scoop from Mitchell Bainbridge about his son who plays lead guitar for this heavy metal band in Austin. He just had both nipples pierced." Wally rubbed his chest. "It hurts me just to think about it."

"You and me both." Deb wiped a trickle of sweat and tried to ignore the way her own nipples, still sensitive after Jimmy's fierce suckling, rasped against her bra as she leaned down and rummaged in her bottom drawer for a pair of spare panty hose. She'd snagged hers on a prickly bush near the swimming pool.

It was hot all right, and not just because of the temperature.

"Did anybody call for me?" she asked as she unearthed several packs of gum, a spare toothbrush and a minican of mousse.

Wally produced a stack of messages and excitement zigzagged up her spine. "Let's see... Mayor's office—Shirly Wilburn got a promotion from mayor's secretary to city secretary. Chase Gunthrie—his heifer took first place in the Austin County beef finals. Arlene Merriweather—her daughter-in-law just gave birth to triplets. Pastor Marley—he wants to propose a weekly inspirational column at your lunch meeting today. And Titus Langley—he's going for the record again."

Again, as in ten tries to break the state record for spitting the biggest lougie.

So much for excitement.

Deb tried to stifle her disappointment as she rifled through the messages Wally handed her. "Are you sure this is all?"

"Took 'em myself. You waiting on something important?"

Monumental. Thanks to Jimmy Mission, she was sexually frustrated and hot and eager and hot and irritated and hot and… "Not really."

"Because the Texas AP doesn't bother with phone calls. They notify all nominees by certified mail."

"Thanks for clearing that up. Now I can stop waiting with baited breath for the phone to ring." *If only*.

"Be a smart-ass all you want, but the waiting is killing you," Wally told her, "and you know it."

"The only thing killing me is this heat." She sorted the slips of paper and handed a few back to Wally. It was better that Jimmy hadn't called today. She had appointments all day. Her gaze shifted to the clock. One of which she was late for right now.

She found the panty hose, sent up a silent thank-you because as hot as it was, she wasn't about to show up to meet Pastor Marley without a pair on. She was shameless in some ways, but not with a man who had a direct connection to the head honcho upstairs.

"You cover Titus on your way to Chase Gunthrie's," she told Wally as she headed for the storage room and a private place to change. The only bathroom was out in the hallway directly above Pancake World, and as hot as a furnace this time of day. "I'm going to meet Pastor Marley, then I'm off to the old Blake place—Mr. Blake's put out three brushfires in the past week and I wanted to get an interview to go with the heat wave theme. Arlene's place is on the way, so I'll handle her. After that, I'll swing by the Piggly Wiggly."

"How come I have to cover Titus?"

"Because he's on the way to Gunthrie's and there's no reason for us to waste time." At Wally's knowing stare, Deb shrugged. "Titus has already ruined four pairs of my heels, two pairs of panty hose and a silk skirt." While the farmer could spit some whoppers, he had terrible aim. "This is my last spare pair, not to mention, I'm wearing my favorite Italian pumps."

"I'm wearing tennis shoes," Paige offered, pushing up her eyeglasses and coming around the desk where she'd been sitting quietly. "And I've even got galoshes at home."

Deb turned on the timid woman. "You think you're ready for an assignment?"

Paige adjusted the eyeglasses again, squared her shoulders and nodded. "As ready as I'll ever be. Besides, you guys have a lot to do. I'm almost done with this copy. I'll run it down to the basement with the other finished pieces. Then there's no reason I can't help out. All I need is a lift over to Moby's service station to get my car."

"I'll drop you off," Deb offered. "Just let me change."

"And I'll head on out." Wally snatched up his camera and notepad. "Catch you guys later."

He disappeared and Paige headed down to the basement while Deb went into the back room to unbutton her skirt and step free. She was wrinkled enough without having to hike the linen up to her armpits and fight with a damp pair of hose.

She'd just draped her skirt over a nearby chair, peeled off her ruined stockings and was pulling the new ones from the package when she heard the door creak open.

"I'm almost done—" She started as she turned, expecting to find an anxious Paige.

Instead, she came face-to-face with Jimmy Mission.

Faded denim hugged his thighs. A red T-shirt clung to his muscular torso, outlining broad shoulders. Short sleeves revealed tanned biceps that rippled as he tipped his hat and gave her that damnable grin that never failed to rob her of speech.

"Hey, there, Slick. I had some free time and I thought I'd stop by and see what you're doing for lunch." His gaze roved over her and the devil himself danced in his wicked green eyes. "You hungry?"

And how. Her heartbeat quickened and the air paused in her lungs for a long, drawn out second before reality hit her—she was standing there wearing nothing but a pair of silk bikini panties and a blouse, a pair of hose dangling from her fingers.

She ignored the sudden urge to snatch up her skirt and run for cover. "Didn't anyone ever teach you how to knock?"

"The door was open."

"You should have knocked anyway."

"And spoil the surprise?"

"What surprise?"

"Me." He kicked the door shut behind him and reached her in two strides. "I didn't sleep much last night."

She licked her lips and tilted her head back, her gaze skimming the strong, tanned column of his throat, his firm jaw and sensual lips, to the bright green eyes that glittered down at her. "The horse keep you up late?"

"You kept me up, darlin'. All night." He leaned down, his breath feathering her lips. "I couldn't stop thinking about where we left off. Here." He feathered his lips over hers. "And here." His strong fingertips slid beneath her blouse, skimmed her rib cage and cradled her breast. "And here." His thumb stroked her nipple over her bra and heat bolted through her.

"And here," she breathed, catching his hand and urging it down over her bare belly. Strong fingertips grazed the elastic of her panties and her breath caught, her eyes closed.

"Ah, Slick, you're so—"

"Deb?" Paige's voice sounded on the other side of the door, followed by a timid knock. "I'm back and ready to go."

His hands stilled as he stared down at her. "I'm guessing this is bad timing."

"The worst. Pastor Marley is waiting for me. We're having lunch."

"I thought you didn't know Pastor Marley."

"I don't. I'm interviewing him over chicken-fried steak at Pancake World."

His hands slowly fell away. "Then I guess you'd better get to work, Slick."

She came so close to throwing herself into his arms and forgetting all about the pastor and the heat wave and Arlene and the Piggly Wiggly.

Wait a second. Forget her work? Her livelihood? On account of a man?

The realization sent a spurt of fear through her and suddenly she was thankful for the interruption. She needed to breathe some air that didn't smell like warm, sexy male with a hint of leather and outdoors.

As if on cue, Paige's voice sounded from the other side of the door again. "Deb? You okay?"

"I'll be right there," she called out. She stepped into her skirt, stuffed the pair of hose into her pocket and slid on her shoes. "We'll have to finish this later."

"You can count on it."

His words followed her to the door and lingered in her head long after she'd escaped into the cool air-conditioning of her car, Paige chatting away next to her.

A promise that she knew Jimmy Mission would keep. The question was *when?*

5

By the time Deb finished her last interview, she was ready to go into major meltdown. Images of Jimmy, that cocky grin on his handsome face and the passionate gleam in his eyes, had haunted her throughout the day. That coupled with the fact that they were in the middle of one of the worst heat waves to hit Texas in years made for nearly unbearable conditions.

She slid the third button free on her blouse. Her fingertips feathered over the heart-shaped tattoo and Jimmy's voice slid into her mind.

This has been driving me crazy all morning.

Her nipples pebbled at the memory, the anticipation. Soon, she promised herself as she turned off the main road and headed for the Mission Ranch. Very soon.

She'd caught Jimmy at a bad time last night, and he'd made the same mistake today.

No more.

It was Saturday night and most every cowboy that worked the Mission ranch had already headed off to BJ's for a little slip and slide on the dance floor. Deb had it on good authority—namely, Dolores, who was never wrong when it came to other people's business—that Jimmy's mother would be attending Saturday night bingo with the rest of her seniors' group from the church. That meant an empty house and plenty of privacy for the Texas-size chicken-fried steak she'd picked up at Simpson's diner. Her gaze hooked on the box of edible undies sitting in the passenger seat and she smiled. Steak followed by a little strawberry dessert, of course.

Anticipation rippled through her along with a shiver of excitement as an old Rod Stewart song echoed through her head.

"Tonight's the Night."

"HEY, COWBOY," Deb called out when she caught sight of Jimmy as he sauntered in the opposite direction toward the barn.

He wore an old brown work shirt, the sleeves rolled up to midbicep, a pair of faded brown chaps strapped around his worn jeans. He came to a dead stop at the sound of her voice. His muscles tensed, but he didn't turn.

"What are you doing here?"

She came up behind him, stopping a few feet away as she stared at the broad expanse of his back. The setting sun outlined his shape, making him seem larger, more powerful, and heat skittered up her spine. "I brought dinner and a little dessert. I thought you might be—why don't you turn around?"

"Tell me you're not naked and I might consider it."

"What are you talking about?"

"The past few times we've met up, you've been minus clothes. The first time in the bridal shop, you were half-naked. Last night you were completely naked. Today half-naked. If history's any indication, it's likely you're standing there without a stitch on and that means there's no way in heaven, hell or the in-between that I'm turning around."

A wave of self-consciousness swept through her. *Self-consciousness?* Of all the weak, ridiculous emotions. She stiffened. "Because you don't want to see me naked?"

"Because you're liable to end up flat on your back with a dirty, smelly cowboy on top of you, one who's hard-pressed to round up a batch of strays. I can't afford a distraction now."

His words sent a burst of heat through her that had nothing to do with the steamy weather and everything to do with the sudden image of a certain dirty, smelly cowboy pressing down on her, into her.

She forced a deep breath and watched the muscles in Jimmy's arms ripple as he flexed his fingers, as if it took everything he had *not* to turn around. A strange sense of triumph rushed through her because she affected him as much as he affected her.

"We moved a herd of cows from the north to the south pasture and lost a few along the way," he went on. "I give my cowboys Saturday nights off, so that leaves me to find the strays before sunset." Silence ticked by for several seconds. "So?" he finally murmured as if he couldn't help himself. "Are you?"

"Am I what?"

"Naked?"

She smiled. Despite his refusal to look, there was an unmistakable thread of hope in his voice. "You'd better move those cows, Hoss."

"You *are* naked, aren't you?"

"Bye, Jimmy."

So much for Rod Stewart, Deb thought as she turned and headed for her car. Tonight definitely called for the Rolling Stones, because it seemed that, no matter how she tried, Deb Strickland could get no satisfaction.

SHE COULDN'T have been naked.

Jimmy told himself that for the hundredth time as he urged his horse around a crying calf that had gotten separated from his momma and urged the animal toward the rest of the herd.

She'd been standing out in the middle of his ranch, in front of God and everybody who happened along, in broad daylight. Naked?

Nah. That was pushing the envelope, even for Deb. She had no way of really knowing who she might happen upon.

Then again...

He remembered the suggestive hint in her voice and the sweet smell of her standing so close behind him, all soft curves and warm woman. His body hardened in response and he realized then that it didn't matter whether or not she'd been naked. She'd let him think it, and his damned thoughts were nearly as powerful as the real thing.

He forced aside the image of Deb wearing nothing but red high heels and a pair of edible strawberry undies.

"Giddyup!" He pushed the strays toward the herd, putting all his energy into maneuvering his horse.

He finished up quicker than he expected, the sun barely starting to set by the time he started back toward the barn.

His muscles ached and sweat poured off him and he wanted nothing more than to step into a hot shower, fill his stomach with some of his mother's apple pie—she was practicing for Inspiration's annual pie festival being held later this week—and finish up the stack of invoices waiting on his desk.

Like hell. There was one thing he wanted more.

A sudden image of a woman with long, dark hair and creamy skin and the sweetest, most intoxicating mouth he'd ever seen flashed in his head and sent heat pulsing to all the wrong parts, distracting him from his exhaustion, from his duty, from every-thing....

Slow and easy.

As much as he wanted her, he had responsibilities. He'd had a few extra hours today and he'd been in town, so seeing her had been convenient. Tonight wasn't, and while they had an agreement, Jimmy couldn't just chuck everything like some sex-crazed fifteen-year-old because the prettiest girl in class had shown up and offered him dinner.

And dessert.

His heart pounded faster at the thought and forced him to take a deep breath. Hell, it was nearly dark. By the time he made it back and showered and changed, it would be too late to go to town. Jimmy had to be up early tomorrow.

He had to be up early every day.

Before he could give in to the near overwhelming urge to push the horse faster, jump a few fences and hightail it into Inspiration, to hell with a shower and a change of clothes, he turned Emmaline around and galloped back across the pasture, to a thick stretch of trees.

No man had ever died from a bad case of lust. That's what he told himself as he pushed the horse further until he reached the familiar old cabin.

He slid from the saddle, wincing as his throbbing groin grazed the saddle horn. Then again, there was a first time for everything.

DEB'S HIT-AND-MISS out at the ranch turned out to be an omen of things to come.

Sunday morning, Jimmy showed up at her place for breakfast, but she was already climbing into Paige's old Impala to help the girl find a decent place to live. Sunday night, Deb headed out to Jimmy's and found herself smack-dab in the middle of the church ladies' weekly prayer meeting; it was his mother's turn to host. Deb had made up an excuse about covering the meeting for the newspaper, joined hands and prayed. Prayed for the strength to ignore the cowboy grinning at her from the doorway. His presence had made her heart thud and her face flush so badly the group's president, Martha Sue Jenkins, had called the fire department and reported the town's first case of heatstroke.

Monday, Jimmy had driven to Austin to meet with a prospective breeder for his prized bull, Valentino, while Deb had dealt with the typical beginning-of-the-week disasters: her printing press wouldn't print, Wally called in sick and Paige spent the morning bickering with a mortgage company while Deb did triple the work.

Tuesday, Jimmy was busy with his herd while Deb followed an ancient set of instructions on how to repair her aging printing press because Wally was still laid up with a case of summer flu.

Wednesday evening, they happened to meet at a fundraising hoedown for the Blakes, the family whose house had been partially destroyed by fire thanks to the lack of rain and the dangerous temperatures. They'd barely exchanged hellos before the mayor had walked in with his three twenty-something nieces who'd rushed straight over to Jimmy. He'd ended up doing everything from a fast two-step to the Cotton-Eyed Joe, while Deb had sipped punch, glared and wished she'd penned a different Fun Girl Fact this week. Something like *Try a little subtlety*, rather than the edible undie suggestion. While she had nothing against a woman going after what she wanted, the way some of the girls around town literally threw themselves at Jimmy, made her heart ache for womankind everywhere. To be that desperate...

Deb would *never* be that hard up for a man.

Okay, so maybe in the physical sense. After all, she was a healthy, fully functional woman and she had needs. But a husband? No way. Even if that prospective husband were Jimmy.

Especially if it were him.

Not that Deb had to worry about marriage with him. Jimmy didn't desire her in that way. His smiling agreement to dance with each of the mayor's nieces proved that. Nor did Deb desire him in that way, which was why she'd turned him down when he'd asked her to dance.

Their relationship was—would be—strictly sex.

FRIDAY MORNING rolled around and still no sex.

The truth echoed through Deb's head as she stood inside the local VFW hall and did a quick visual search for Jimmy.

Of course, he wasn't there. He was probably out branding cows or doing some other macho-rancher

thing, while she was here suffering from a major case
of deprivation.

"I really don't have time for this," Annie said as
she came up next to Deb. "I've got a million things to
do and barely two weeks to do it all."

"That's the point. You still have to find someone to
do the cake, so here you go." Deb motioned toward
the rows of booths.

"This is the annual pie festival. There isn't a wedding cake in sight."

"The best bakers in the county are right here in this
room. Not to mention, those very same bakers are the
ones who enter the fried chicken festival and the barbecue cook-off and the chili catillion. You've yet to
find someone to make cocktail weenies and all that
other stuff for the reception. Here's your chance to
find a caterer without doing the traditional appointments and interviews. It's like a megamall. One-stop
shopping."

Annie eyed a nearby chocolate fudge pie and its
proud mama, Emily Gentry, who also served up the
best meatloaf at the town's diner and made a mean
Italian cream cake. "You do have a point."

"And you've got about two hours before I promised to have you at the flower shop to look at bridal
bouquets. Now get to work and start sampling."

Seeing prospective taste buds, Emily motioned
them forward. "I've got just what you need right
here, girls. This stuff is so rich, it's better than sex."

"I'll take this one," Deb said, reaching for the offered sample.

Annie grinned. "I thought I was the one doing the
tasting."

"As official maid of honor, it's my duty to help."

She sampled the chocolate and heaven exploded on her tongue. For a few blissful moments, she forgot the ache between her thighs and the frustration that had kept her tossing and turning last night.

"So?" Emily eyed her.

"I think I need another slice to really form a solid opinion." She handed her cup back over and the woman cut a thin sliver. "Better make that two," Deb added. "I've got slow taste buds."

"How's the dress coming?" Annie asked a few moments later around a mouthful of chocolate crème.

"Fine." Or it would be as soon as Deb managed to push Jimmy Mission from her thoughts and concentrate on the blasted thing.

"When can I see it?"

"Soon—why, would you look at that," she said, effectively killing any further talk on the subject as she drew Annie's attention to the pride of Inspiration's annual pie festival—a six foot tall rendition of the Alamo made entirely of stacked tarts, complete with a lattice crust for the surrounding wall and a courtyard full of chocolate army men. "Boy, would I like to take a bite out of Davy Crockett."

Deb had finished off Davy, Santa Anna and at least a half dozen unknown soldiers and gone back for another piece of Emily's chocolate sex when she heard the familiar voice behind her.

"Hey, there, Slick."

She whirled, her mouth full of pie, and stared up at Jimmy Mission looking tall and handsome and delectable in faded jeans and a white T-shirt.

And hungry. He definitely looked hungry. Particularly when his gaze hooked on the corner of her mouth and he reached out, skimming a spot of chocolate cream with his fingertip. His thumb grazed her lip and her heart slammed to a halt for a long moment as his touch lingered. She watched, mesmerized, as he licked the tip of his finger.

"It's not chocolate body paint, but I guess it'll do."

She managed to swallow. "What are you doing here?"

"Dropping off my mom." He motioned to the main entrance to the hall and the woman standing at the registration table. "She's entered every year since I was a kid."

"I figured you'd be off herding cows."

"I will be in about a half hour. Until then, I'm eating pie. What about you?"

"The proverbial killing two birds. I'm covering the event for the paper and Annie needs to find a caterer. So..." She searched for something, *anything* to distract her from the heat of his gaze and the need coiling inside her. "Do you like pie?"

He grinned. "Everything from lemon meringue to apple to chocolate." His gaze darkened as it hooked on her lips. "Especially chocolate. When the craving hits me, it's a little hard to control."

Her attention shifted to his mouth. He had such firm lips, yet soft at the same time when they touched hers just so.... "I know the feeling," she blurted.

"Do you, now?" He leaned closer, his sweet breath feathering her lips.

Too close, her common sense whispered, urging her to step back. If only her darned feet would cooperate.

"What are you doing?" she asked when he leaned even closer, angling his head.

"I need a kiss."

"Here?" There were sure to be repercussions if he

kissed her now in front of everyone. A serious, responsible, family-oriented man like Jimmy didn't single out a female he had no long-term interest in unless he wanted to be the subject of a major gossip fest. While Deb prided herself on being no stranger to scandal, for some insane reason she didn't want people speculating about her relationship with Jimmy.

Or her lack of.

"Stop," she blurted.

"I'm not doing anything," he said a heartbeat away, his breath feathering her lips and making them tingle. "Not yet."

Okay, so maybe just one—

"Deb!" Annie's voice rang out from a nearby table and jumpstarted Deb's common sense. "I need you."

Jimmy drew in a deep breath, as if to gather his control. "If I didn't know better, I'd say we're cursed. You didn't tell the pastor what we're up to, did you?"

"I had one interview with him, and I didn't say a word about what was up, because so far, you've been too busy, I've been too busy, the world's been too demanding, so nothing's up."

"Speak for yourself."

Her gaze dropped and she noticed that he was, indeed, *up*. Her cheeks heated and need rushed through her. She managed a quick "See you later," shoved a spoonful of Chocolate Dream into her mouth and turned on her heel, before she stripped off her clothes and threw herself into Jimmy Mission's arms.

You are not that desperate.

Not yet, anyway.

"I REALIZE that this is a major event in your life, Mrs. Franklin, but your hamster having her litter really isn't the sort of thing we like to include in the What's Up With Folks column." Deb clutched the receiver and listened to the excited voice on the other end late Friday afternoon. "It belongs in the What's Up With Pets section." Deb managed to say goodbye and hang up. She turned and caught Wally's stare.

"We don't have a What's Up With Pets section," he said.

"We do now."

He grinned before turning to Paige. "Eskimo pie."

Deb stiffened and turned to the article on her desk about that morning's pie competition, and the jumbo-size Chocolate Dream pie she'd purchased after a frustrating half hour watching Jimmy sample the goodies. The way his lips moved around each bite, the way he licked his fork and smiled at her whenever he caught her eye across the crowded room. Her stomach grumbled at the memory, along with her hormones, and she shoveled a forkful of sweetness into her mouth, praying it would satisfy both.

"For your information," she said after she'd swallowed. "This has nothing to do with how excited Mrs. Franklin sounded or the fact that Fluffy endured fourteen hours of labor and deserves at least a mention. It's business."

Wally grinned. "Sure, boss."

"Smart-ass." Deb devoured another bite and caught Wally's stare.

"Are you feeling all right?" he asked.

"Fine," she said around a mouthful. "Why?"

"You've eaten half that pie."

"And?"

"You haven't once complained about your hips. I

mean, you eat junk like everybody else, but it doesn't go down quietly."

Paige, wearing her typical large swallow-up-everything T-shirt and overalls, shoved her glasses back on as if to get a better look at Deb. "Are you worried about something?"

The question drew Dolores's interested gaze from across the room. The old woman eyed her over a pair of bifocals. "Worried? You're worried, dear?"

"I am not worried."

"It could be nerves making you act so out of character," Paige went on.

"It isn't nerves."

"Maybe you're angry," Wally suggested.

"Or sad," Paige added.

"Or excited," Dolores said hopefully.

"Or sexually frustrated."

The last comment slid into her ears, the voice deep and familiar and stirring. Her gaze swiveled to the left, to where Jimmy Mission stood filling up her doorway.

Soft, worn Wranglers caressed his firm thighs, cupped his crotch and covered his long legs. A plaid work shirt framed his broad chest, the top two buttons undone, revealing the smooth, tanned column of his throat and a hint of gold hair. The usual grin curved his sensuous lips, but strangely enough, the expression didn't quite touch his green eyes. Determined eyes.

Her heart stalled and her pulse raced and heat tingled through her. He stepped forward and she made the sign of the cross. "Stay back."

He shrugged. "Not a chance, Slick."

"I've got three articles to finish by five. Three articles I *have* to finish. We go to press first thing in the morning."

"And I've got a few dozen head of cattle that just arrived yesterday."

"So you're busy, too."

"Yep." He reached the desk.

"And I'm busy."

"Yep." He proceeded around the desk.

"And we haven't got time for this."

"Yep." He reached for her hands and pulled her to her feet. His lips caught hers in a quick, rough kiss that made her blood rush and her hormones weep.

Wally whistled.

Paige gasped.

And Dolores said in a breathless voice, "Stop the presses! This definitely qualifies as front-page material."

"Don't even think about it," Deb told the older woman before turning back to the cowboy standing so close and smelling so sweet. "Jimmy, I—" The words faded into a squeal as he leaned down and she found herself folded over one broad shoulder.

"What are you doing?"

"Picking you up. You're in charge, son," he told Wally as he headed for the door.

"Sure thing."

Deb caught an upside down glimpse of Wally's smiling face as she grasped the door handle. "You'll do no such thing. I'm in charge. I'm..." The words faded as the door frame slipped from her hands and he took the stairs with a haste that surprised her.

"I can't believe you just did that in front of my staff."

"Since when do you care what people think?"

"They're not people. They're my staff. You're crazy."

"Damn straight." Boots crunched gravel as he headed across the back parking lot. "I can't eat or sleep or concentrate and it's your fault, and it's about to end. We're getting out of here and into a bed, and we're not coming up for air until I can think clearly. So don't even think about putting up a fuss."

Metal clicked as he unlocked his Bronco, hauled open the door and hefted her onto the seat next to a few jars of what looked like chocolate fudge sauce.

"What's this?" She fingered one of the containers tied with red-and-white gingham ribbon.

"Inspiration's version of chocolate body paint fresh from the kitchen of Pancake World via Kerry Michaels."

Her gaze shifted to the window and the woman currently eyeing Jimmy as she served up an armful of plates to one of the tables. "The head waitress?"

"She missed me a few weeks back when you wrote *Pump him up with chocolate body paint,* and so she's just now getting around to giving it to me." He pinned her with a stare. "You're making my life miserable, you know that?"

"Am I?" A smile tugged at her lips.

"Don't look so damned happy about it." His expression went from fierce to desperate and something softened inside her, because Jimmy wasn't a man to look fierce or desperate. "I'm through waiting, so don't even think about arguing." He shut her door, rounded the truck and climbed in. Upholstery creaked, his door slammed closed.

"You're not thinking about arguing, are you?" he asked after a long, silent second.

The question warmed her even more than the sticky seat and suffocating air because, despite his macho show, he wasn't going to force her into something she didn't want.

She smiled and fingered a gingham-decorated jar. "Actually, I'm thinking that I've got a sudden craving for chocolate."

6

JIMMY HAD MEANT to take her to a motel.

At least that's the idea that had been simmering in his head since they'd first agreed to get together. A private room at a nice, discreet place just outside of town where they could get on with their business without any interruptions. An idea that had finally boiled over after an entire week of sleepless nights, topped off by an afternoon of horse breeding the old-fashioned way.

A guy could only take so much.

He'd left Wayne in charge of the breeding session, taken a shower, made a quick reservation at the Star-light Inn and hopped into his Bronco to fetch Deb, the world be damned. For a little while anyway. For the good of the ranch.

He was too preoccupied, too uptight and much too frustrated. He wasn't getting near the work done that he should have. He needed some relief. He needed her. Now.

So he'd opted for the quickest solution instead, turned off the main road and driven them here, strictly for convenience sake. It certainly wasn't because he wanted her to see his cabin, to actually like it. And no way was it because he'd been fantasizing about seeing her in his bed for more months than he

could count. They could get together anywhere as far
as he was concerned.

This, he told himself again as he stared at the newly
built cabin visible just beyond the break between two
towering Texas pines, was nothing more than pure
convenience.

"This isn't a motel," she said, her gaze following
his.

Jimmy didn't have the heart to look at her, to see
the disappointment in her eyes and so he busied himself killing the engine and climbing from the front
seat.

"I know it's not much," he said as he rounded the
front. "Just something I've been building in my spare
time." He helped her from the passenger seat and
started walking toward the cabin. "It's still a work in
progress, but the walls are up and it has all the bare
necessities to get us through the night. Lights and
running water and a shower and—"

"It's really big." her voice sounded behind him as
she followed.

"—and the toilet is fully functional—"

"And isolated."

"—and there's a king-size bed with fresh sheets
and—"

"And nice."

"—and there's a new stove in the kitchen—what
did you say?" He stopped and turned on her so fast
she bumped into his chest.

"I said it's nice." Her gaze met his and, for a split
second, Jimmy could have sworn he saw a glimmer
of admiration. A strange warmth spread through
him, a feeling he quickly pushed back down when he
noticed her shoes.

Her attention followed his and she picked up her feet, dislodging one of her heels which had sunk a few inches. "Nice, but messy."

"We could drive up to the motel if that's what you really want?"

She cast a glance past him and something strangely close to longing flashed in her eyes before fading into hard, glittering determination. She planted her hands on her hips. "If you're trying to weasel out of our agreement, you can just forget it. I haven't spent the past ten minutes holding this jar of chocolate syrup for nothing." She indicated the container in her hands. "Time to pay the fiddler."

He quirked an eyebrow at her, a grin tugging at his lips. "Slick, *you're* the one who owes *me*."

Surprise raced across her features, followed by an irritation evident in the narrowing of her luscious lips, as if the truth had just dawned on her and she wasn't a bit pleased that she'd forgotten it. "In that case, I'd better get to work."

Before he could so much as blink, her free hand reached out and gripped his collar as she hauled him close for a kiss.

SEX, DEB TOLD HERSELF, throwing herself into the single act of kissing Jimmy Mission, desperate to ignore the strange feelings that had assailed her the moment they'd rolled to a stop in front of the cabin—the sprawling, still-under-construction cabin with the hand-carved porch swing hanging out front. One look at the swing and she'd had a sudden vision of herself, barefoot and pregnant, rocking back and forth, Jimmy next to her.

It wasn't the vision that had bothered her so much,

but her reaction to the vision—the surge of tenderness, the desperation, the longing.

To be barefoot and pregnant? With Jimmy?

No way. She'd vowed off marriage and babies a long time ago when she'd walked away from Houston and the man her father had picked for her. A man who hadn't loved her half as much as he'd loved her family's business. A man she hadn't loved at all.

Not that love had ever figured into the picture when it had come to her father. He hadn't had time for such soft emotions. Living a good life that involved responsibility and discipline and keeping up appearances had been all that had mattered to him, and exactly what he'd expected from each of his five children.

Her brothers had delivered in spades. While they'd all been bold and outrageous in their own right, they'd never gone against their father's wishes. He'd wanted sons to follow in his footsteps, and they'd done just that. Robert, the oldest, ran the paper her father had just acquired in Dallas. Danny, ran the affiliate in Amarillo. Chuck, the *San Antonio Sun*. And Bart, the youngest, served as VP at the *Houston Chronicle*.

Deb had been carrying on the grand family tradition herself, being the docile, demure, conservative daughter her father had wanted her to be...until her granny Lily had passed on and she'd realized how fast things could change. Life was too short to waste, pretending to be something she wasn't.

Pretending, instead of really living.

She wasn't going back to Houston, and she wasn't falling for any man, no matter how many porch swings he had hanging outside his cabin. Or how good he kissed. Or how he pulled her close and rubbed the base of her spine with his thumb until she wanted to melt onto her back and purr. Or how he held her close, his arms solid and strong and possessive, as if she actually meant more to him than a few moments of pleasure.

This wasn't about forever. It was about this moment, this kiss, *this...*

The jar of chocolate syrup thudded to the ground, quickly forgotten as her arms locked around his neck.

For the next few moments, she drank in the taste and feel of him, ran her hands up and down his solid arms, relished the ripple of muscle as he cupped her buttocks and pulled her closer.

He rocked her, his hardness pressing into her and heat flowered low in her belly, spreading from one nerve ending to the next until every inch of her body burned.

She moaned into his mouth and, without breaking the kiss, he swung her into his arms, retrieved the jar of chocolate and headed for the cabin.

A few seconds later, her feet touched down in the bedroom. The walls were still raw and unfinished, just bare frame filled with insulation, except for one. Floor-length windows spanned from corner to corner, overlooking the surrounding forest and a small lake that shimmered in the distance. A large king-size bed, piled neatly with colorful quilts, sat in the middle of the floor, looking out of place amid the surrounding chaos of wood and tools. Beams crisscrossed the ceiling, framing a tarp-covered square—a soon-to-be skylight. Sawdust covered the floors and as much as Deb liked the soft floral scent of her potpourri-scented bedroom, she found herself inhaling, filling her lungs with the sharp aroma of fresh air and Texas pine and Jimmy.

He set the jar of chocolate on the nightstand before turning to her. She flew into his arms and kissed him again, the need building until she clawed at his clothing. He caught her wrists and pulled back, his grin slow and wicked and wolfish.

"We've got all night, Slick."

All night? Was he deranged? Her heart pounded, her blood rushed, her body ached and wanted and... "Five minutes," she blurted as she unfastened her skirt and let the material pool at her ankles. "I'll give you five minutes, then if you don't start undressing, I'm ripping it all off of you."

"Five minutes, huh?" A blond brow quirked as his dark, heated gaze slid from hers to roam down her body—her parted lips and heaving chest and quivering thighs—and back up again.

Impatience flashed in his eyes, or so she thought. But the hands that slid from her shoulders to her collarbone, and down, were strong and sure and slow. Wickedly slow.

"I think I'd rather undress you first." Through the thin fabric of her blouse, he traced the slope of her breasts, changing course just shy of actually touching her nipples—throbbing, aching nipples that whimpered when his fingers caressed her sensitive breasts and cupped their fullness.

"You're not undressing," she pointed out, breathless and needy. "You're touching."

"I like touching."

"But don't you think it would be better if there weren't all these clothes in the way?"

"Maybe." His hands skimmed her bare thighs and heat sizzled along her nerve endings.

"One down and four to go," she breathed.

"You weren't kidding about the five minutes, were you?"

"You've just wasted another ten seconds with that question."

His grin widened. "Then I guess I'd better stop talking and get busy." He did, his movements quick and sure and controlled.

That was the thing about Jimmy. He was always in control, always flashing that same cocky grin, staring at her with those teasing green eyes. Even now, despite the swiftness with which he unbuttoned her blouse, she sensed that he was still holding himself in check. Still the same old smiling, teasing Jimmy.

The realization bothered her a lot more than it should have.

But then he parted her blouse and touched her, his hot fingertips tracing the edge of her bra where lace met skin, and she forgot everything except the need churning inside her.

Deb's eyes closed on a moan and she tilted her head back, arching her chest forward. Strong fingers stroked her nipples through the lace for several long moments until she gasped.

"Two," she croaked.

A deep male chuckle warmed her skin a heartbeat before his hot mouth touched her neck, licking and nibbling as his hands worked at her bra clasp. A few tugs and the lace cups fell away.

She all but screamed at the first stroke of his callused thumb over her bare breast. The next several moments passed in a dizzying blur as he plucked and rolled her sensitive nipples, until they were red and ripe and aching for more.

"Three," she managed as his hands slid down, skimming her rib cage and warming her stomach.

There was no chuckle this time, just a deep male growl when his hands slid into her panties and found her wet and ready. One fingertip parted her swollen flesh and dipped inside.

"Five," she cried, grabbing at his shoulders, clutching fabric as she fought to feel his bare skin against her own.

"What happened to four?"

"Who cares? Just take off your shirt. Please."

Surprisingly, he didn't taunt or tease. He leaned back far enough and let her peel the material up and over his head. She tossed the T-shirt and went for his jeans, but he'd beaten her to the punch, his tanned fingers working at the zipper.

Metal grated and the jeans sagged onto his hips. He stepped back far enough to push them down and kick them free until he stood before her wearing only a pair of white briefs. He was rock hard beneath the soft white cotton. A heartbeat later, the full length of him sprang forward, huge and greedy, as he pushed his underwear down and kicked it to the side.

But it wasn't the sight of him naked and tanned and fully aroused that took her breath away, it was the heat burning in his gaze, making his eyes a bright fierce green.

Her hands went to her open blouse, but he pushed her fingers aside to peel the shirt and bra away from her flushed skin.

"Aren't you forgetting something?" she breathed when he made no move to remove her last item of clothing—a pair of slinky bikini panties cut high on the thighs.

"Hold your horses, woman. I was just getting to it." He cupped her, his palm warm through the thin covering.

An ache flowered low in her belly. "Get to it quicker."

"You definitely need to learn a little patience. Haven't you ever heard the saying good things come to those who wait?"

"Idle hands are the devil's plaything," she breathed, the phrase ending on a low moan as he traced a finger along the elastic edge between her legs.

"Haste makes waste." He dipped one finger past the elastic, into the steamy heat between her legs. "And I don't want to waste a minute of this." He stroked and teased and a sweet pressure tightened low in her belly.

"You, um—" her teeth sank into her bottom lip as she struggled for her own control "—you've got a point."

"Then it's settled. We're not going to rush this." For emphasis, he slid his finger into her slowly, tantalizingly, stirring every nerve to vibrant awareness until he was as deep as he could go, and then he withdrew at the same leisurely pace. Advance, retreat, until her heart pounded so hard and her breath came so fast, she thought she would hyperventilate. She was close. So close...

"Not yet," he murmured, withdrawing his hand before dropping to his knees in front of her.

He touched his mouth to her navel, dipped his tongue inside and slid his hands around to cup her bottom for a long moment before moving his mouth lower. His tongue dipped under the waistband of her panties. He licked her bare flesh before drawing back to drag his mouth over her lace-covered mound. His lips feathered a kiss over ground zero and her legs buckled. Her hands went to his bare shoulders to keep her from falling.

A warm chuckle sent shivers down the insides of her thighs before he lifted his head and caught the waistband of her underwear with his teeth. He drew the material down, lips and teeth skimming her bare flesh in a delicious friction that made her want to scream. Her entire body trembled by the time she stepped free.

"My turn."

"I don't have any underwear on." He pushed to his feet and faced her.

"I'll improvise." She knelt and kissed his navel, swirling her tongue and relishing the deep male groan that vibrated the air around them. She grasped him in her hand, running her palm down the length of his erection. He was hot and hard and she did what she'd been wanting to do ever since she'd seen him standing there completely nude. She took him into her mouth and laved him with her tongue as a low hiss issued from between his lips.

He grasped her head, his fingers splaying in her hair, guiding her, urging her—

"Stop." The word was little more than a groan before he pulled her to her feet and tumbled her down on the bed.

She watched as he withdrew a foil packet from his jeans pocket and put on a condom in what she estimated had to be some sort of record time.

"I thought you wanted slow," she said as he settled himself between her thighs, his penis pressing into her a delicious inch.

"I changed my mind," he muttered, as if the realization bothered him. Before she could comment, he pressed her thighs wider, grasped her hips and slid into her with one deep thrust.

He stilled for a long moment, letting her feel every pulsing vibrating inch of him as he filled her completely.

She closed her eyes, fighting back the sudden tears that threatened to overwhelm her. This was crazy. This was sex. It was all about feeling good, not about *feeling*.

"Are you okay?" His voice was soft and deep and so tender she had to fight back another wave of tears.

Tears, of all the silly, ridiculous...

She swallowed and forced her voice past the lump in her throat. "Are you going to talk or move, cowboy?"

His mouth opened and she thought he was going to make a smart comeback, but then he dipped his head and his lips closed over her nipple. Thankfully. She needed a distraction from the strange feelings threatening to overwhelm her.

Mmm...

All thought faded into a wave of delicious pressure as he suckled her long and hard, his erection pulsing inside her. The sensation of him drawing on her breast and her body drawing on his was nearly unbearable. And then he moved, pumping into her, pushing her higher—stroke after stroke—until she cried out, her nails digging into his back as she climaxed.

Several frantic heartbeats later, her eyelids fluttered open just in time to see him throw his head back, his eyes clamped tightly shut. He thrust deep one final time and stiffened, every muscle in his body going rigid. Her name tumbled from his lips, riding a raw moan of pure male satisfaction.

He collapsed beside her and gathered her close, pulling her back against him in spoon fashion. His chest was solid against her back, his arms strong and powerful around her. Warmth seeped through her, lulling her heartbeat for the next several minutes as their bodies cooled.

Her gaze went to the floor-length windows and the sparkling lake just beyond. The setting sun sent a dance of orange brilliance across the shimmering surface.

"Wow," she breathed, the word so soft and hushed she marveled when she heard his deep voice in response.

"You should see it on a clear, moonlit night."

"How did you ever find this place?"

"My dad and I used to come up here fishing when I was just about knee-high. Jack was still clinging to my momma's skirts instead of tagging along after me and so it was just the two of us." He nuzzled her neck. "Dad was always so busy, but he still found time to bring me up here on Saturday afternoons. This was the first place I came to after my dad's funeral. I still couldn't believe it. I walked around out here and half expected to see him come whistling up the path, his fishing pole hooked over one arm."

The sadness in his voice touched someplace deep inside her and before she could think better of it, her hand settled over his where he anchored her waist.

"When I walked into the *In Touch* office after my granny Lily passed away, I swore I could still smell her perfume." Now why had she said that? Because it was so warm and he smelled so good and it was hard to think straight with her hormones still in a tizzy after breaking such a long fast. At least that's what Deb told herself. "Even now, if I close my eyes and take a deep breath, it's as if she's right there."

"You loved her a lot, didn't you?"

"She was the only person that I could ever really talk to."

"What about your folks?"

"My mother passed away when I was a little girl and my father was never long on understanding." She expected the mention of her father to stir the usual loneliness, but with Jimmy's arms around her and his lips so close to her ear, she didn't feel alone. She felt warm and wanted and content, and she realized in a startling instant that she liked having Jimmy curled around her as much as she'd liked having him deep inside. Maybe more.

"We're not finished yet, are we?" she blurted, desperate for a quick distraction from the crazy feelings.

Before she could blink, she found herself yanked onto her back. Jimmy glared down at her for a long moment as if the comment actually bothered him. Ridiculous, of course, because nothing she said or did seemed to *really* bother him. They argued and bickered, yet he always managed to stay so cool and aloof and charming.

Until now.

His expression eased, quickly killing her theory as a slow, sensual smile crept across his lips.

"Nah, Slick. That," he said, pausing to kiss her

heart-shaped tattoo and one pert nipple, "was just the warm-up." He slid down her body, his large hands going to the inside of her thighs. He spread her legs wide and scorched her with a heated glance before reaching for the jar of chocolate body paint. Unscrewing the lid, he retrieved a dollop and rubbed it between her legs with an exquisite swipe of his fingers before giving her that damnable grin. "The main event starts now." And then he dipped his head, lapped the chocolate-drenched folds with his tongue, and provided a much needed diversion from the tender feelings coiling inside her.

She didn't want tender. She wanted wild and wicked and hot. And for the rest of the night, that's exactly what he gave her.

UGH. SHE WAS NOT a morning person.

Deb promptly shut her eyes against the first rays of sunlight peeking over the horizon. She made it a point never to leave her house before three cups of coffee and a full hour spent with some mascara, a good lipstick and a dozen hot rollers.

Judging by the delicious aroma filling the cabin, Jimmy definitely had a coffeepot, but she'd lay down her next manicure that he was fresh out of all the rest.

She took a deep breath and contemplated making a run for the bathroom. She could at least fingercomb her hair and rinse her mouth out and stall for a few more minutes before she had to face him after the shameless way she'd responded to him last night. *All* night.

Shameless is your middle name, she reminded herself.

True, but this was different. Jimmy was different. He made her feel…*things.*

Of course, he did. He made her feel excited, frustrated, hot—end of story. And she wasn't bolting for the bathroom like some shy teenager who'd just told the high-school stud that she had a crush on him. After all, she'd licked chocolate body paint off the man. The least she could do was face him.

"Good mor—" The rest of the greeting died in her throat as she turned and found an empty bed. After a frantic search through the partially built cabin, she realized that Jimmy Mission had ditched her. She found only his keys along with a note instructing her to take his truck back to town—he would pick it up later— and to drive safely.

To make matters worse, she wasn't the least bit relieved, despite that she had a rat's nest sitting on her head. Instead, disappointment rushed through her, along with a healthy dose of irritation. Drive safely? That was all he could say after she'd given him the best night of her life?

Her irritation ballooned into anger when she padded into the kitchen and realized he'd left barely a quarter inch of coffee in the pot. Not even enough to whet her tastebuds and what's more, the coffee can was empty.

That settled it. She was killing him. As soon as she headed home, had her regular dose of morning coffee and pulled herself together in the form of a shower and some heavy-duty hair and makeup, she was going to find the nearest shotgun, hunt down Jimmy Mission, and put him out of her misery.

That is, if she didn't break down and kiss him first.

7

"YOU LOOK like you could use this." Nell set a cup of coffee in front of Jimmy when he walked into the kitchen just after sunup. "Heck, you look like you could use a whole pot."

Amen. He needed another shot of caffeine, of *something*, to zap his brain and focus his attention on anything besides how sweet Deb Strickland smelled or how soft her skin was or how tempted he'd been to stay in bed with her.

Tempted, but he hadn't given in. He had a ranch to run and so he'd hightailed it out before she opened her big blue eyes and he found himself hell-bent on losing himself in her hot little body just one more time.

"Not sleeping well?" Nell asked as Jimmy finished off his first cup and poured another.

"I slept just fine." The few minutes he *had* slept.

"Hmmph," she snorted. "You'll have to explain that one to me, because it just don't figure."

"What doesn't figure?"

"You sleeping fine when it's as plain as the stubble on your face that that bed of yours hasn't been touched, not to mention you've got them tired circles under your eyes."

"Who's tired?" The question came from his mother as she walked into the kitchen fully dressed in a pink pantsuit and her good pearl earrings, despite that it was only a few minutes past daybreak.

"Jimmy," Nell told her. "He didn't sleep in his bed last night."

"The bed *upstairs*," he quickly clarified. "I was hammering up Sheetrock at the cabin and it got late, so I bunked out there."

"So you weren't here at all?" He nodded, expecting his mother's eyes to fire even brighter with worry. Instead, relief flooded her features. "That's good. I mean, not good that you were gone," she rushed on as if eager to explain, "but you did get some sleep. That's the most important thing."

"I'll probably be sleeping there for the next week or so. We're clearing the south pasture and it's closer if I just crash there instead of riding all the way back here. Speaking of which..." He pushed his chair back from the table. "Daylight's burning."

"Jimmy," his mother started, "since you're here, I think it might be a good idea if we talk. The sewing circle met yesterday after the pie competition and—"

"No time." He bolted to his feet. Talking was not a good idea because Jimmy didn't want to lie and no way was he telling his mother that he'd propositioned Deb Strickland for sex. That he'd spent the first of two weeks' worth of nights with her. That he couldn't wait for the next night. "Wayne's waiting."

"But I was chatting with Mildred Cook and she said—"

"How is Mrs. Cook?" he cut in as he snatched up a piece of French toast and a napkin. "I haven't seen her in ages."

"Just fine. She said—"

"She still have those gallstones?" He ate half the toast and reached for the Thermos Nell had filled.

"They were kidney stones and she had surgery last year over at the county hospital. I saw her yesterday and she said—"

"And she lived to tell about it?" Without waiting for a reply, he rushed on, "You wouldn't catch me going to County unless I was this close to giving up the ghost." He kissed his mom on the cheek and started for the door. "Later, ma."

"But—" The door closed on the rest of his mother's sentence and Jimmy didn't waste a second getting the hell out of there.

The sewing circle was really a cover for the senior ladies' weekly gossip fest, of which Jimmy had no doubt he'd been the prime subject, particularly after kidnapping Deb from the newspaper office in front of nosy Dolores Guiness. His mother had probably had a dozen phone calls by now and she wanted an explanation.

But he sure as hell couldn't explain his relationship with Deb when he wasn't too clear on it himself.

Not clear? Wait a second. He was clear, all right. Damn straight. His take on the situation was as transparent as the freshwater creek bed up near Bentley Hollow. His relationship was purely physical, even if he had been tempted, damned tempted to stay in bed with her that morning.

He stuffed the Thermos into his saddlebag and mounted up, keenly aware of the time because he *had* stayed in bed with her a half hour longer than he'd intended. His ranch hands had been out in the north pasture since daybreak while he'd been tangled up with the sweetest, softest, warmest—

He cut off the thought before it could get him into real trouble. Before the memory of Deb Strickland's naked, tempting body could push its way into his head and distract him the way the real thing had distracted him early that morning. He had a ranch to run and he didn't have time for such foolish daydreams. He'd wasted enough time on his dreams. His life was about work now, about building up the ranch and taking care of his land, and building a family with someone who didn't have balls bigger than his own.

He ignored the grin that twitched at his mouth and urged his horse to a gallop. Grin? Hell, no, he didn't feel like grinning. Deb was more trouble than she was worth and it was a good thing—a *damned* good thing—he wouldn't have to put up with her for too long.

Just two weeks. Two weeks of her soft, kissable lips, her silky-smooth skin, her warm, inviting body....

"Yo, Boss! You lose your sense of direction?"

The voice startled Jimmy from his thoughts and back to reality and the all-important fact that his foreman had ridden up next to him and they were now both headed north.

North? Christ, he was supposed to be *less* distracted now that he'd gotten Deb Strickland into his bed.

"There's a whole mess of ranch hands waiting in the south pasture. We are clearing the south, right? 'Cause I could have sworn that's what you said."

"Um, yeah. I was just giving Emmaline here a little exercise." He ignored Wayne's doubtful look, pulled his horse around and started in the right direction. "Let's get to work."

One week and six days.

He could make it until then, until the affair ended and Jimmy worked her completely out of his system. Besides, with each day that passed, each *night*, the situation was bound to get easier. He was crazy as a loon now because his system was in shock. A long period of abstinence followed by hot, bone-melting sex was bound to fry any man's brain. But sex was like beer, as far as Jimmy was concerned. There was nothing more tempting than an ice-cold can dripping with condensation after a long, hot day spent outside. The liquid never failed to go down as smooth as silk and make him crave more. But by the time he finished the second, his thirst was somewhat sated and he wasn't nearly as anxious to pop the tab and guzzle another. It would be the same way with Deb. Each night with her would curb his thirst for more, until he woke up one morning and that was that. Lust sated. Craving satisfied.

Until then he intended to keep his compass handy.

IT WASN'T a gun, but it would do.

Deb's fingers flexed on the spray nozzle as she sighted her target clear across the small parking lot where the elementary school was holding its annual car wash, which she'd helped organize.

Only because she'd needed a story for her Neighbors Helping Neighbors section, she reminded herself. Her volunteering on a Saturday when she should have been working had nothing to do with the fact that the proceeds were going to repair the cracked slab on the playground pavement, courtesy of the current Texas heat wave, where poor little Amber Carmichael had fallen and sprained her ankle. This was all about business. And those color books she'd dropped by Amber's house this morning had been good PR.

And this—her fingers flexed around the handle of the water hose—*this* was payback.

Squinting against the late afternoon sunlight, she took aim. A little to the left... Now a tad to the right... *There.* Squeezing the trigger, she smiled with evil satisfaction as a stream of water flew over the heads of several first-graders busily washing the mayor's 1953 Cadillac and nailed Jimmy Mission right between his sexy green eyes. He'd shown up a few minutes ago in search of his truck, which she'd parked near the parking lot entrance—bait to lure him to the car wash and give her a chance at revenge.

After several hours and too many cars, she'd come close to giving up on him. But just when she'd been ready to call it a day and head home to change her damp blouse and skirt—Deb did everything dressed to the hilt—she'd seen Wayne's Chevy roll into the parking lot, Jimmy in the passenger seat. He'd climbed out and started toward her, barely covering a few feet before three teachers had cornered him— three single teachers clutching what looked suspiciously like jars full of chocolate syrup.

Now three single *wet* teachers.

Deb ignored Jimmy and the trio of angry women and went on about her business of washing the left headlight of Pastor Marley's classic powder blue Thunderbird.

Her heart pounded for several furious heartbeats while she contemplated various possibilities for next week's Fun Fact, until the sound of boots crunching gravel grew too loud to ignore and a shadow fell across hers.

"You did that on purpose," came the deep, accusing voice. Water dripped onto the ground near the toe of one of Deb's favorite blue pumps and satisfaction swept through her.

"I don't know what you're talking about." Deb tried her best to look innocent. Not an easy task for a woman who made it her business never to look innocent.

He pinned her with a knowing green stare. "You fired that water hose at me on purpose."

"What water hose?"

"The one in your hand, Slick."

"You mean this one?" She held up the spray nozzle as if seeing it for the first time.

"You squirted me on purpose."

"I did no such thing."

"You sure as shootin' did."

"No, I didn't." She fired the nozzle and gave him a quick squirt in the face. "Now I've squirted *you* on purpose. A few minutes ago, I squirted you *and* your fan club."

His eyes flashed green fire for a second as he wiped his dripping face, but then a grin curved his sensuous lips. "You wouldn't happen to be suffering from a little green-eyed monster, now would you?"

Damn straight.

Deb forced the unsettling thought aside. "I am not jealous. I'm mad." She pinned him with an accusing glare. "You drank all the coffee this morning."

"Coffee?" His grin widened. "You went ballistic with a water hose over coffee?"

"I did not go ballistic. I just got you a little wet."

"A little?" He arched an eyebrow at her, amusement dancing in his green eyes before they darkened and the air stalled in her lungs. "I'm soaked to the bone in case you haven't noticed."

She'd noticed, all right. His white T-shirt, now practically transparent, stuck to him like a second skin, showing off every bulge and ripple of his broad shoulders and muscular chest. She could even see the shadow of hair that circled his nipples and funneled down his abdomen. "And it looks like the condition's contagious."

She became acutely aware of the glide of water down her neck, the sticky wetness of her silk blouse plastered against her chest. A glance down and she realized her own clothing was in no better shape than his, her shirt practically transparent, revealing the lacy bra she wore and the puckered tips of her breasts.

"You look good wet." His deep voice stirred something even worse than the sudden panic beating at her senses. Excitement flowered inside her, making her heart pound and her blood rush. She felt herself melting beneath the warmth in his eyes, his smile, and so she did what any freedom-loving woman would have done. She squirted him again for good measure, turned on her heel and walked away.

Actually, she practically *ran*.

This feeling was not part of her plan. Having fun, getting some exercise, reinforcing her already tarnished reputation—all on her agenda. But this warm, achy feeling? Over reliable, home-and-hearth-loving, coffee-hoarding Jimmy Mission?

No. No matter how hot the temperature, how hot

his gaze, or how hot the heat that burned between them. This was strictly sex.

Unfortunately, despite her reputation, she wasn't used to strictly sex. She wasn't used to *any* sex, which explained why she couldn't forget Jimmy or his damnable grin the rest of that afternoon after she finished up at the car wash and headed to the *In Touch.*

"You and Jimmy," Dolores clucked the moment she walked in. "I never would have guessed."

"There is no me and Jimmy."

"He kissed you yesterday."

"So?"

"And threw you over his shoulder." The older woman gave an excited quiver. "Just like Tarzan."

"First off, it was just a kiss. It didn't mean anything and Jimmy's about as far from Tarzan as a man can get." Jimmy was a man in control. He took things slow and steady and thorough. It was Deb who'd been begging and screaming and pounding her chest from all the wonderful sensations he'd stirred last night. "And I don't expect a word of what happened here last night to leave this office."

Dolores pouted. "Not even a juicy tidbit at the bottom of my column?"

"Not one single word."

"So much for freedom of the press," the old woman grumbled as she gathered up her purse. "I'm off to a dinner. Hopefully I'll hear something even juicier than you and—" The words died at Deb's stern look. "You and no one. No kiss. No Tarzan."

"That goes for the rest of you," Deb told Wally and Paige.

"What kiss?" Wally asked.

"I, personally, think Tarzan's an overrated mass of

testosterone," Paige added. "We need more sensitive men in the world."

Deb turned her attention to her work—last-minute edits and a stubborn printing press and the general worry that came with meeting her weekly deadline. Unfortunately, it wasn't enough to make her forget Jimmy.

He was there in her head, teasing and tempting and reminding her of last night. Of how much she still wanted him.

"So there I was and I thought, why not?" Paige's voice pushed into her thoughts sometime later. "I deserve this. I do, don't I?"

"What?" Deb took a deep, calming breath and tried to focus on the young woman.

"The community college." Paige indicated the course booklet in her hand. "I was over in Jasper running an errand for Wally—more ink for the press—and I stopped at a convenience store and right next to the newspapers was this course book, so I picked one up. I was thinking about taking a few classes in the fall." Uncertainty flashed in her green eyes. "I mean, that is, if I can find the time and my work schedule permits." She turned the booklet over in her hands, a wistful expression on her face. "Woodrow and I got married while I was still in high school. He wanted me to quit, but I talked him into letting me take classes at night. I got my diploma by mail."

"Good for you. But it's a shame he felt that way."

She blinked, as if fighting back tears. "It is. At the time, I thought he was just being protective. That's what he told me—how he wanted to take care of me, to keep me safe—but it was all just bunk. He didn't want a wife, he wanted a slave to keep his house and cook his dinner. He cut out everything in my life that didn't directly involve him, and I let him because I believed him. Because I loved him. As much as I wanted to go to college, I also wanted to have a family. To live the fairy tale. To stay at home and keep his house and raise his babies." Her gaze dropped to her hands. "That's probably hard for you to understand."

She thought of last night and the vision she'd had of herself barefoot and pregnant. "Maybe not as hard as you think."

Paige stared at her for a thoughtful moment before she asked, "Anyone I know?"

Jimmy. The name rushed to the tip of her tongue, but she managed to hold it back. *Strictly sex.* He'd awakened her long-deprived hormones and so, of course, he was starring in a few crazy fantasies. But that's all they were. No way did Deb actually *want* to be barefoot and pregnant. She hadn't spent years cultivating her taste in shoes to give them up now. She was merely suffering from a bad case of lust.

"I was speaking figuratively," she told Paige. "I'm a reporter, so naturally I'm sympathetic to the human condition. It makes my work more real." She grabbed a stack of ad sheets and put on her most intimidating glare. "Take these down to Wally for me."

"Um, sure," Paige said, the uncertainty that always filled her gaze rushing back in full force. "I didn't mean to insinuate that you... I mean, I thought you might want to talk about it and I..." She nibbled her bottom lip and shoved her glasses back up onto her nose. "I know you're busy, so I'll just take these." She snatched up the sheets and turned to flee, her baggy T-shirt and overalls rustling with each step.

"I think the community college is a wonderful idea," Deb said, drawing the woman back around. "You owe it to yourself, and don't worry about your job. We're flexible here. Just let me know your schedule and we'll work around it."

"You'd do that for me?" Hope glimmered in her eyes and a strange warmth unfurled inside Deb.

She frowned. "Strictly for the good of the newspaper. We need intelligent, informed people working here, that's all." A knowing light glimmered in Paige's eyes and Deb added, "If you say I'm an Eskimo pie you're fired."

"You're an ice queen."

"You'll go far in this business."

Deb, on the other hand, was about to flush her own career down the toilet if she didn't get on the ball and think. She had all of five minutes to come up with a Fun Fact for the next issue before she missed her deadline.

Think.

It should have been easy. Her Bitchy, Bold & Beautiful mug was filled to the brim with steaming black coffee. Her favorite CD played on a nearby player. All was right with the world. All she had to do was jot something down, anything. Anything that didn't involve food and an ungodly amount of calories and...

An idea struck and her pen went to work for several frantic seconds.... There. That was it. Sexy and fun, minus the food and calories, because her hips couldn't take much more after last night's batch of homemade body paint.

Not that she was going to demonstrate this Fun Fact for Jimmy Mission, the slug. Not after he'd hogged all the coffee and accused her of being jealous.

She was *not* giving him any demonstrations.

OKAY, so maybe she'd do one teeny, tiny demonstration.

She stared down at the burgundy canister wrapped in a matching ribbon and bow Jimmy handed her later that evening when he walked into the *In Touch* office after everyone else had left. "You brought me a can of coffee?"

"You said you liked coffee." He stood near the doorway, looking so fresh and delicious in worn jeans and a western shirt, his hair damp from a shower, his jaw newly shaven. A memory rushed at her, of that same jaw stubbled with a day's growth of beard, rubbing and chafing the tender insides of her thighs. Desire bolted through her.

But it wasn't the desire that melted her anger so much as his deep, rumbling voice. "I'm really sorry about this morning."

"I..." She searched for the voice of strength that never, ever failed her. "Yeah," she finally murmured, fighting down the strange surge of warmth that rushed through her as she fingered the bow on his gift.

"If I had known how attached you were to the stuff, I would have left you an entire pot."

She swallowed the sudden lump in her throat, and came to a monumental decision. "That's all fine and dandy," she said as she placed the gift on her desk, "but that doesn't help me tonight."

"You want coffee now?"

"Not exactly." She eyed him. "I want you."

His eyes glittered, mirroring the same desire that rushed through her. "I thought we could head back to my cabin."

"And waste fifteen minutes?" She smiled, took his hand and led him to the center of the room. "Not a chance, cowboy."

"What are you up to?" he asked as she pulled out a chair and pushed him into it.

"Research." She grinned and winked and reached for the buttons on her blouse. "The Fun Girl Fact for the week: Tease him with a little striptease."

Surprise registered in his expression before something deeper and more intense took its place as he watched her slide the buttons on her blouse free. He was a rapt and eager audience for the space of several furious heartbeats, before his gaze swiveled to the side.

"What is that?" His attention riveted on her CD player.

"Not a what. It's a who. Ricky Martin. He's the hottest thing around."

"This is George Strait country, Slick, and he's the hottest thing around here."

"I'm talking hot as in *hot*." She gave her hips a shimmy. "Not hot just in terms of talent." She closed her eyes and swayed to the Latin beat. "This music is steamy. Sexy."

Her eyelids fluttered open a few seconds later to find him once again a rapt audience. She finished undoing the last button on her blouse. The material parted and cool air swept her bare skin, pebbling her nipples and making them press against the lace of her bra, snagging Jimmy's gaze. Deb's heart pounded double-time and she fought down a sudden wave of self-consciousness. She'd been naked in front of him before. She'd had sex with him. It was a little late for the shy routine.

The thing was, it wasn't a routine. Jimmy did, indeed, make her feel shy and naive and innocent and a dozen other ridiculous emotions that carefree, self-proclaimed fun lover Deb Strickland had no business feeling.

At the same time, he made her want so badly, so fiercely, that nothing else mattered, and so she tuned out everything except the heat, the glitter in his bright green eyes, and the need gripping her body.

With trembling hands, she reached for the clasp of her bra.

As if he noted his effect on her, he murmured, "Careful, honey. I'm liable to think you haven't done this before."

"Are you kidding? A fun lover like me? I've done this dozens of times. Hundreds."

"Really?"

No. "Sure."

He leaned back, as if settling in to watch the show and folded his arms. "Then wow me with some of the finer points of taking it all off."

"Well, first off, you need some hot music because it's all in the hips." She gave hers another shimmy and watched the fire flare in his eyes. "Point two, always maintain eye contact." A quick twist of her fingers and the clasp unhooked, the lace cups parted and her breasts sprang free. "Now, now," she scolded, when his attention shifted. "You're supposed to maintain eye contact."

"I think," he said, pushing from the chair and clos-

ing the distance to her, "eye contact's highly overrated." He cupped her breasts. "I prefer hands-on."

"But I'm not finished with my striptease. I still have
the bottom half to go."

"Trust me, Slick. You're finished." And then he
claimed her lips in a hot, leisurely probing kiss.

He proceeded to make slow, sweet love to her, first
at the newspaper office, then later back at his cabin,
until Deb was even more firmly convinced that
Jimmy Mission was the best, the most thorough, the
most stirring lover she'd ever had.

He was warm and he was wicked and he was all
hers.

For now.

8

"THAT TAKES CARE of the flowers," Annie told her Sunday morning as they sat having breakfast at Pancake World. She eyed the wedding planner sitting on the table next to a plate of blueberry pancakes. "All that's left is the rehearsal dinner and the dress." A worried gaze met Deb's. "Please tell me I can cross the last one off my list. I haven't been able to sleep all week worrying about everything, and that dress, that *awful* dress, has been at the top of my list."

"Relax. The dress is practically finished."

"Really?"

"Sure." *Not.* And it was all Jimmy Mission's fault. Deb had been so preoccupied with their agreement that she'd forgotten all about the dress.

"Can I see it tomorrow?"

In your dreams was right there on the tip of her tongue. But one look into Annie's eager eyes rimmed with tired circles from nights spent worrying over wedding preparations, and she found herself blurting, "First thing."

Hey, she hadn't taken all those design classes in college for nothing, despite what her father had said.

"Journalism," her father had stressed when he'd finally found out that she'd been sneaking in a few design classes with her regular course load. "We're a journalism family. It's what we do, who we are.

There's ink in our blood, Deborah, yours and mine, and I'll not have you waste your time with such frivolous nonsense that means nothing in the big scheme of things."

From then on, he'd selected her courses himself, and that had been the end of the beginning of her career as a fashion designer.

The end of her career, but not her dreams. She'd still sewn to her heart's content every summer at Granny Lily's, and while her hard work might not have sparked world peace or exposed scandals or kept the world better informed, it wasn't a complete waste. It *did* mean something in the little picture of things.

It meant the world to Annie.

"Tomorrow," she promised her friend. "Now eat up."

After finishing her own breakfast, she headed home to spend her Sunday working on Annie's dress.

"We've got our work cut out for us," she said to Camille after she'd moved the coffee table to the side of the room and laid out the satin and lace nightmare on her living-room floor.

The cat purred her distaste.

"Now, now, I know it's bad, but we can do it."

Camille didn't look convinced as Deb retrieved her ripper and her scissors. She settled crosslegged on the floor—the cat lazing next to her bare thigh, a "Brady Bunch" marathon on some obscure cable channel—and went to work.

By the time evening rolled around, her neck was stiff, her arms felt this close to falling off, and she'd more than earned the carton of ice cream sitting in her freezer. She'd just collapsed onto her couch, fixed her

gaze on Mr. and Mrs. Brady as they lectured poor
Marcia about boys, and shoveled a spoonful into her
mouth when the doorbell rang.

A few heartbeats later, she found Jimmy Mission
standing on her doorstep in faded jeans and a denim
shirt, his straw Resistol sitting on top of his blond
head. The porch light outlined his broad frame and
made him seem bigger and more intimidating. Or
maybe it was his frown doing that.

"You're supposed to be at my place." His gaze
swept the length of her, from her bare toes covered
with red nail polish, up over bare legs and her slinky
robe, to her face. "We have an agreement."

She nailed him with a glare, doing her best to ignore the warmth that his gaze stirred. "Who says I'm
supposed to be at your place? We didn't lay down
any ground rules."

"Then let's lay some down. You and me. Every
night for the duration of two weeks."

"That's one week and five days. We've already
used up two."

"One week and five days," he reaffirmed. "I'll pick
you up after work."

"Smack dab in front of Dolores Guiness? I don't
think so. I had to lie my way out of our kiss the night
before last. While she bought that story, she's not
likely to buy another if you keep showing up."

He arched an eyebrow. "You scared of a little scandal?"

"I live for scandal. You're the one with something
to lose. Every mama in this town wants you for a son-
in-law. Being seen with me is sure to ruin your reputation. You'll be scraping rock bottom for a farmgirl."

"I want a ranch wife, not a farmgirl."

"Whatever. It's better if I meet you somewhere."

"Where?"

They needed quiet and discreet and... "The cabin. I'll meet you every night after sundown at your cabin. Every night except for tonight. I'm busy." She tried to shut the door, but he'd planted his boot firmly between the door and jamb.

"Doing what?" he persisted.

"None of your business."

He leaned against the door frame and folded his arms, his boot still wedged in her doorway. "I can stand here all night."

She shrugged. "Oh, all right." She stepped back and opened the door so that he could see the living room and the white creation spread out on the floor. "I'm working on Annie's dress. I promised her it would be ready by tomorrow morning."

Some unnameable something flashed in his eyes. Pleasure? Relief? *If only.*

He rubbed his hands together. "Then I guess we'd better get to work."

"I really don't think that's a good idea." She didn't need Jimmy sitting in her living room, distracting her, no matter how appealing the thought.

"Afraid you won't be able to resist my charm?"

Bingo. "Tonight isn't about charm. I really have to finish this. I promised Annie."

"Then I promise to be on my best behavior."

He looked so sincere that she heard herself saying, "I do have to take off all the appliqués on the train. It would certainly go faster with an extra ripper hard at work. But you have to swear to be careful. If you rip the material, then I'll have to patch it and that will take more time."

"Careful's my middle name, Slick." He moved past her, his arm brushing the tip of her breast through the silk of her robe. Heat bubbled inside and she caught a gasp just before it slid past her lips.

Not tonight.

After making that firm vow, she closed the door and watched him survey the dress as if sizing up an ornery cow.

"First question," he finally said. "Where's the ripper?"

She retrieved the small hook-like device from her sewing box, keenly aware of his gaze on her as she moved across the room. "Here you go."

He stared at the object in hand. "Second question." His gaze collided with hers. "What's a ripper?"

A grin tugged at her mouth. "It's used to rip stitches."

He nodded. "Makes sense. So where do I start?"

She was this close to pointing to a particular appliqué when she felt his gaze again, stroking up her bare legs. Heat sizzled along her nerve endings along with a strange sensation that had nothing to do with the way he was looking at her and everything to do with the fact that he was standing in her living room, offering to help her sew, of all things. And she liked the situation far more than any independent, self-sufficient woman should have.

"You're looking at me."

"So?"

"So don't look at me."

"It's just looking. I'm not doing anything."

"You're trying to get into my pants."

"Darlin'." His gaze collided with hers and her breath hitched in her chest. "You're not wearing any pants. You're wearing a robe. And, for the record, there wouldn't be any trying involved. If I wanted you out of that thing, you'd be out in a heartbeat."

"I really don't have time for this." She concentrated on rummaging through her sewing kit, eager to find her extra ripper and her tape measure, and where was a thimble when you really needed—

"But I don't," his deep voice rumbled behind her.

She whirled to find him standing a fraction away, so close that if she drew in a deep breath, the tips of her breasts would kiss the hard wall of his chest.

"I don't want you out of this robe, that is," he went on. "I mean, I do. I'd be lying if I said I didn't." His fingertips touched her thigh just below the hem of her robe. His lips feathered over hers for a brief, warm second before his hand fell away and his fingers clenched into a fist. "But you promised Annie a dress, and I promised you some help, and I always keep my promises, provided you put on some decent clothes." His gaze swept her, from the hard tips of her breasts to her bare toes curled into the carpet. "Sixty seconds," he vowed, putting his back to her as he turned his attention to the dress.

Part of Deb wanted to stay put just to see if he really was a man of his word, but she'd promised Annie. What's more, the idea of having Jimmy Mission in her living room for something other than sex made her heart pound almost as much as the thought of kissing him.

Ugh. She'd definitely watched too many Brady reruns.

She bypassed an old pair of shorts and a faded tank top in favor of a sundress dotted with tiny hearts that matched the one on her right breast. There was nothing wrong with looking nice once in a while. Especially with a hunky cowboy sitting smack-dab in her living room.

"THAT'S NOT exactly what I had in mind." Jimmy stared at Deb who stood in the entryway to the living room and tried to calm his suddenly pounding heart.

She glanced down, as if noticing her appearance for the first time. "You said to get dressed and this *is* a dress."

"That's a matter of opinion." It looked more like a slip. It was short, barely falling to midthigh. The clingy heart-dotted fabric hugged every curve as she stepped toward him.

The real kicker, though, was the simplicity of the getup. No panty hose or high heels. She was barefoot, her legs smooth and tanned, with hardly a hint of makeup on her face, and he wanted her just as much as when she was dressed to the nines.

One tiny spaghetti strap inched down the curve of her shoulder and his fingers itched to reach forward and push the strap back up again.

Or pull it all the way down.

"Jimmy?"

"Uh, yeah?" He shook away the lustful images filling his head.

"Are you okay?"

"Sure thing." He struggled for a deep, calming breath and turned his attention to a much safer subject—the wedding gown. "We'd better get to work." Just to bolster his defenses, Jimmy sat down on the opposite side of the dress. With a few feet between them, he was sure to keep his head and his control.

A FEW FEET wasn't nearly enough.

Jimmy came to that conclusion after several hours of sitting across from Deb, smelling her sweet scent, listening to the sound of her even breathing. Despite the distance, he'd never felt quite so close to a woman...and so at home.

"How'd you learn to do that?" he blurted, eager to distract himself from the dangerous thoughts.

"What you really mean is how did a high-maintenance woman like me—" her gaze caught his "—learn something as self-sufficient as this." She shrugged. "My granny Lily taught me. Our first project, we made a skirt. This awful red skirt with uneven seams and a lopsided waistband." A grin tugged at her lips and his stomach hollowed out. "It was terrible and I knew it, but my granny Lily acted as if it was the most beautiful thing in the world."

"Sounds like her. She was a nice woman."

She nodded, her eyes suddenly bright. "You should have seen her oohing and ahhing over how well I cut the pattern. I never would have tried again if it hadn't been for her telling me I could do it. I never would have come here." At Jimmy's questioning glance, she added, "She always told me I could do anything I wanted to do, be anything I wanted to be. She gave me the courage to try things, to walk away from my father and my fiancé before I made the biggest mistake of my life."

The news stopped him cold. His gaze collided with hers. "You were engaged?"

"Fancy that, huh?" She laughed, but there was a sadness in the sound that made his chest tighten. "He was an all right guy. Sort of cute. Very smart. But the biggest selling point—he came from a Dallas newspaper family. That's what cinched the deal when he popped the question to my father and asked for my hand."

"Did you love him?"

"I hardly knew him." A sad smile touched her mouth and Jimmy had his first glimpse of a softer Deb Strickland. One whose lips quivered and eyes brightened when she spoke of her past. "I told my father as much, but it didn't matter. 'You'll do as you're told, Deborah Elizabeth,' was all he said to me—all he ever said to me while I was growing up." She sniffled. "I'd be married right now if my granny Lily hadn't fallen and broken her hip." She shook her head. "She needed me and so I canceled the wedding which had only been a few days away and came here to nurse her back to health. My father ranted and raved and threatened me not to leave. He didn't care about my granny Lily, just his newspaper." She sniffled. "So I walked away and I haven't been back. I talk to my brothers occasionally, send Christmas cards, but I haven't seen them or my father—especially my father."

"Has he tried to contact you?"

"No. He would never do that even if he wanted to. It's a matter of pride."

He gave her a knowing look. "Must run in the family."

"If he wanted to talk, he would have called me."

"Or you could call him."

Fear flashed in her eyes before she shook her head. "Can we just get back to the sewing?"

He thought about pursuing the subject, but he didn't want her to close herself off to him, not when she'd just begun to open up. He liked listening to her. He liked it far too much.

"So your granny liked your awful skirt?"

She nodded, her face brightening at the change of subject. "And I've been sewing like a madwoman ever since. I've always loved making things. The entire process, from cutting the fabric to actually piecing it together. It all fascinates me. Crazy, huh?"

"Not really." Not to a man whose heart raced at the prospect of cutting fresh Texas pine, of shaping and sanding and hammering until he had a new door or a chair or a table—something he'd made all by himself.

"You're a really good carpenter, Jimmy," she told him as if she'd read the thoughts racing through his mind.

He quickly stifled the pleasure that swelled inside him at her comment. "I'm a rancher, not a carpenter."

"You could have fooled me."

"I fooled myself for a long time," he told her because as much as he liked listening to her, he liked talking to her, as well. Especially when she stared at him with those big blue eyes. Interested eyes. As if she cared about everything that was coming out of his mouth. "I left Inspiration because I felt like I was missing out. I wanted to open my eyes in the morning and see more than a wide-open stretch of pasture and a herd of cows, so I left and joined the marines. After my tour of duty, I settled in Houston. Me and a buddy of mine went into business together. The construction business."

"So you *were* a carpenter."

"Head contractor and crew boss."

She raised her eyebrows. "Sounds like a fancy name for a carpenter."

He grinned. "There were education opportunities in the marines. Anyway, my partner solicited business, while I handled the design and construction. We did pretty well."

"And?"

"And now I'm here."

"What about your business?"

He stiffened. "The ranch is my business."

"Your construction business," she prodded. "You didn't just walk away, did you?"

"That's exactly what I did. What I should have done a long time ago. My daddy worked day in and day out to be able to have something to pass on to me and my brother. The least I can do is take care of the place."

"What about your brother? Where is he?"

"New Mexico, last I heard. He's training horses on a horse ranch. He likes horses. And women. He's been married twice and divorced three times."

"I'm no rocket scientist, but isn't there something wrong with that equation?"

He grinned. "I've been trying to figure it out myself, but no luck. He calls every month or so just to keep in touch, but he's never been much of a talker or much for responsibility."

She gazed at him, her blue eyes twinkling and some of the anger coiling tight inside him eased. "Unlike you. Good ol' reliable Jimmy."

"I've been known to be reliable a time or two, and I'm definitely good, darlin'. But I resent the old part." He held her gaze for a long moment and if he hadn't known better, he would have sworn he saw a flash of longing. Not physical longing, but something that went much deeper and made him want to reach out and pull her into his arms and simply hold her.

"How long has it been since you've seen your brother?" Her question distracted him from the feelings rushing through him.

"My father's funeral."

"That's too long for family to be apart." The melancholy crept back into her expression and stirred a protective instinct inside him that made him want to chase the look from her eyes.

"That explains it then," he declared.

"What?"

"I've been wondering what in the world was responsible for it, and now I know."

"Know what?"

"You see, there's always a reason for these things."

"*What?*"

"Why you're so bossy. Being raised with four older brothers is sure to bring out the worst in a woman."

The sadness disappeared. Her eyes fired with indignation, and Jimmy knew he'd hit a bull's-eye. "I am not bossy." She yanked on her side of the dress and adjusted it in her lap.

"Are, too." He yanked back enough to see her eyes flare.

"Am not." She tugged it her way.

"Bossy," he quipped, tugging at the dress again, only to have her tug back harder. He let loose this time and she sprawled backward. "And sassy," he added as she scrambled upright. "And I like both."

The fierce glare she hit him with lasted all of five seconds before her lips hinted at a smile. The sight warmed him even more than the sexual tension heating the air around them.

"You're one charming man, Jimmy Mission." She seated herself. "Too bad you don't sew half as fast as you talk."

"These hands may be slow, but they're thorough."

Silence settled around them as they both fixed their attention on the dress and tried to ignore the heat sparking between them. "I had a crush on you, you know," she finally said after a long moment, her gaze fixed on the needle and thread in her hands. "That time you opened the door for me at the ice-cream shop way back when. I took one look at you and from then on out, I made Granny Lily take me by the ice-cream shop every time I was in town, just hoping I'd get a glimpse of you."

He remembered all the times he'd seen her, lusted after her in her fancy clothes and shoes. But he'd been just a country boy and she'd been everything he'd never had and always wanted. "Why didn't you say something?"

"You were older and, at that time, I lived in fear of *Big Brothers*."

"You mean Big Brother."

"Not in my case. I've got four, remember? They would have had a major fit had they discovered I was lusting after a boy at the tender age of fourteen when I should have been playing with my paper dolls."

"You don't strike me as the paper-doll type. Too tame."

"Not now, but once upon a time."

They spent the next few hours talking about their childhoods, about their lives in Inspiration, their families. He told her about growing up, about all the trouble he and his brother and Tack used to get into. In return, she told him about being the only female in a household of domineering men. And while she claimed leaving was the best thing she'd ever done, there was a sadness in her voice. Regret.

A feeling he knew all too well...but not for long. Jimmy was burying his past mistakes and doing the right thing, and he wasn't kissing Deb Strickland tonight. No matter how sexy she looked in the heart-dotted sundress or how vulnerable as she nibbled on her bottom lip. No matter how much he wanted to.

HE *WASN'T KISSING HER*, he told himself when he opened his eyes just before the crack of dawn and found Deb lying in his arms on the sofa, her head nestled in the crook of his shoulder, Annie's dress piled next to them. Her luscious breasts pressed against his side. One long leg draped over his thigh, her pelvis nestled against his hip. One of her hands curled between them while the other had crept under his T-shirt. She snuggled deeper into his embrace and a surge of warmth went through him, followed by guilt.

Guilt? It wasn't as if he'd kissed her. He was just holding her. There was a big difference. Monumental. The trouble was, he was enjoying the holding even more than the kissing.

Sex, Jimmy reminded himself. This thing between them was all about getting naked and sweaty and burning off steam. About painting Deb from head to toe with chocolate body paint, then licking her clean one inch at a time.

But, boy, this felt good, too. She felt good. So soft and warm and...*right*.

He forced the thought away as he gingerly moved her hand and inched from the sofa. If he didn't touch her, he wouldn't be the least bit tempted to wake her up with a fierce kiss or suckle her partially exposed breast or gather her into his arms and simply hold her for a few more minutes.

The last thought sent Jimmy scrambling for his boots because Deb Strickland wasn't the sort of woman a man could let himself get too comfortable with.

That's what he told himself as he headed back to the ranch and ducked into the barn to avoid his mother, clearly visible in the kitchen window despite the ungodly hour. He could drink coffee later when the coast was clear. Right now, he needed to get to work because Jimmy valued home and hearth and his legacy, while Deb relished her freedom.

Jimmy knew why he felt a connection to her that went beyond lust. Deb reminded him of the man he used to be, of the success he'd achieved and the wild life he'd lived and the satin sheets he'd been so fond of. She was everything he'd left behind in Houston, and it was only natural that he'd feel a sort of camaraderie with her.

That's what Jimmy told himself as he saddled up and headed out for another long, exhausting day. Now if he only believed it.

9

"YOU MISSED your true calling." Annie stared at her reflection in Deb's bedroom on Monday morning and fingered the white satin skirt, now free of butterfly appliqués. "It's absolutely beautiful."

"You're beautiful. This—" Deb circled her and picked a few pieces of wayward thread from one sleeve "—is just a dress."

Nothing in the big scheme of things. Inconsequential.

"A gorgeous dress," Annie corrected, a tear sliding from her eyes. "You turned a disaster into something wonderful. I don't know how I can ever thank you."

Deb handed her friend a Kleenex and blinked away her own tears. "Honey, you just did. Now dry up. This is a happy occasion."

Annie sniffled and smiled. "You're right. I don't know what's wrong with me."

"You're getting married at the end of next week, that's what's wrong." Deb started undoing buttons and helping Annie from the dress.

"At least now I can relax a little bit— Oh, no!" Her gaze swiveled toward the clock sitting on Deb's mantel. "I've got to meet Tack to get the marriage license." She yanked on her clothes and grabbed her purse. "Thanks so much, Deb." She kissed Deb on the cheek and left, dress in hand.

"Now *I* can relax," Deb said, collapsing onto her sofa.

She leaned her head back and closed her eyes, intent on getting a few hours of shut-eye. It was still early in the morning and she'd been up all night and...

Her nostrils flared as she drank in the scent that lingered on her sofa. *Him.*

Anticipation coiled in her stomach. It stayed with her throughout the day as she went about her business and did her best to keep her mind on work.

Fat chance after last night. Talking with him, spending time with him, had only made her want him more and so she called it quits early and headed out to the cabin before the sun had even set.

The place was even more beautiful in the daylight and she took her time walking around. She prowled the porch and watched the play of sunlight off the lake. She trailed her hands over the newly carved front door, fingered the grooves and drank in the smell of fresh wood.

Not only was the craftsmanship exquisite, but Deb had another reason for marveling at the work. It had been done by Jimmy's hands.

"YOU REALLY are talented," she told him later that night when he finally showed up at the cabin and found her sitting on the porch, rocking back and forth in the hand-carved swing. She ran her palm over the smooth lines, a warmth coiling inside her. "And this place is better than nice. I've never seen anything more beautiful." And since it was a moment of truth between them, she couldn't help but add, "And I haven't done hundreds of stripteases. I've only done one. The one I did for you."

He didn't say anything. He simply pulled her from her seat and into his arms, and took her breath away with a deep, probing kiss that lasted several moments before he peeled off her clothes.

"I've never seen anything more beautiful than you," he told her when she finally stood naked before him, the words husky and raw and filled with a strange sense of awe that touched something inside her and robbed her of any quick comeback.

"I think so, too," she said when she managed to find her voice. "That you're beautiful, I mean. A beautiful man. I certainly didn't mean what you meant, which was that I was the one who was—"

"Has anyone ever told you that you talk too much?" he cut in.

"Actually, you—"

He silenced the rest of her response with his lips, his hands sliding around her waist, cupping her buttocks and rubbing her against him until she whimpered with need.

But true to form, Jimmy Mission took his time bringing her to full awareness. The friction of his jeans rubbing against her tender flesh made her gasp and moan and beg.

"I want to be deep inside you, Slick."

"Then *do* something," she gasped, hooking her leg over his hip and rubbing in a shameless, needy gesture. "Anything. Just do it now."

"This?" He cupped her breasts, tugged and rolled her sensitive nipples until she gasped. "Or this?" He swept a hand down her belly and touched her between her legs. His fingers slid into her slick folds, finding her clitoris and plying the swollen tissue until a moan slid past her lips. "Or *this?*" He slid one finger deep inside her and she came close to screaming.

"Which one, Slick?" His husky voice penetrated the roaring in her ears.

"This." She touched his straining erection, stroked the length of him through his jeans and a fierce light flared in his eyes for a brief moment, before the expression eased and she was left to wonder if she'd only imagined it. He slid his hand free of her body and cupped her face for another one of those long, slow, hot kisses.

Lifting her in his arms, he carried her inside and placed her on the bed before stripping off his own clothes. His warm body pressed the length of hers and he took his time making love to her, and when he finally, *finally*, entered her, his movements were slow and controlled and frustrating.

It was as if he held himself back on purpose as he plunged sure and deep, and even though she enjoyed every moment and came to a shattering, screaming release, she couldn't help but imagine what it would be like to have Jimmy completely out of control and wild in her arms. Just once.

She quickly dismissed the notion. If he could have her panting and begging by doing the typical charming cowboy routine, she hated to think what he could do if he actually let go and gave her any real emotion.

She would fall for him in a heartbeat, and Deb had already promised herself not to fall for Jimmy Mission. Regardless of the way he settled next to her after their lovemaking, his chest cradling her back, his arms solid around her waist, one warm palm cradling her breast.

She forced her attention to the window and the lake shimmering in the distance, eager to ignore the warmth creeping through her. The contentment.

"Thank you," he whispered after a long moment, and she knew the words didn't come easily. "Thank you for liking this place."

Something shifted inside her and she couldn't help herself. She smiled. "I wish I could see some of your other work."

"Maybe the next time you're in Houston. I could give you a list of addresses."

"I'm talking about here in Inspiration. It's a small town, but there's always room for a talented builder."

"There's no room in my life to be a builder. I have a ranch to run."

"And you can't run a ranch *and* build if you want? Whatever happened to having it all?"

"That's not an option for me."

"Why not?"

"Because."

"Because why?"

"Because...it just isn't, that's all."

"Well, at least now I understand."

"Because," he growled, pulling her onto her back and leaning over her, "it makes me want more." Surprise registered in his eyes as soon as the words were out, and she knew he hadn't meant to say them. "That part of my life is over and done with. I have to let go completely, otherwise, it's always there, tempting me, calling to me." He closed his eyes and silence ticked by. "It's better to let go," he said at last. "Just let it all go."

"And be miserable? Maybe you're into being a

martyr just to preserve the family business, but not me. That's why I walked away."

"Straight to another newspaper. Just because you're a few more miles away, doesn't make what you're doing any different. You're still following in daddy's footsteps."

"By choice, not because I *have* to. That's the difference. I run the *In Touch* because I like it, not because someone expects it of me."

"Maybe I like ranching." At her knowing look, he collapsed onto his back and stared at the ceiling. "I *do* like it," he said after a long moment. "I remember working cattle with my dad when I was just five years old. We'd start out way before sunup and we wouldn't quit until evening. I loved riding with him. I loved every minute."

"Sounds to me like it isn't the ranching you love, so much as that it reminds you of your dad."

Silence settled around them for a long time before he finally said, "I should have been there when he died. I should have been right beside him. If I had been—"

"—maybe things would have been different," she cut in. "And maybe not."

He seemed to weigh the words for a long moment, before he leaned up on one elbow and eyed her. "Has anyone ever told you you talk too much?"

She grinned. "As a matter of fact, there's a certain cowboy—" He silenced the rest of her words with a long, slow kiss that upped her body temperature.

When he pulled her on top of him and slid her down his hard, rigid length, she was slick and ready. Her body closed around his and she gave herself up to the fire that burned between them.

That night set the stage for the week to come. Deb spent her days at the newspaper office and her nights with Jimmy. He made love to her in his bed, on the porch swing, during a moonlit swim in the river. Afterward, they would talk. About her life and his life and the future. She learned all about his aspirations for the ranch and told him about her plans to improve the newspaper's circulation.

And as one week turned to two, Deb found herself wondering more than once what she was going to miss the most about Jimmy Mission—talking to him or making love with him.

She knew it would be both.

"IT'S HERE." Wally stood in the doorway of the *In Touch* office and waved a white envelope.

"I told you I don't care."

"Sure, you do." He waltzed into the office, passed Paige and Dolores who had both paused in the midst of typing to watch the exchange. "You live for this sort of thing. Competition's in your blood. You're vicious."

"I'm an Eskimo pie, remember?"

"Strictly on a personal level. This is business." He waved the envelope. "Aren't you just a little bit curious?"

"No." Seconds ticked by before her curiosity got the best of her. "Oh, all right. Give it to me." She snatched the envelope from his hand, tore open the seal and pulled the letter free. "Dear Miss Strickland," she read, "We are happy to inform you that the Inspiration *In Touch* has been nominated for Best Weekly in the..." *Best Weekly.* Her own voice echoed in her ears and excitement rushed through her. Her paper had made the cut for Best Weekly.

"What's Best Weekly?" Paige asked.

"Only the biggest honor this little old paper can ever hope to receive. This is the major leagues. The NFL of small-town reporting. It doesn't get any better than this." Wally grabbed the envelope from Deb. "Let's see... The ceremony's in two weeks in Austin. That's a two-hour drive. You'll have to leave early if—"

"I'm not going."

Wally pinned her with a stare. "What do you mean you're not going? You *have* to go. It's nondebateable."

"It's on a Friday night. I can't go traipsing off to Austin when I've got a deadline the next day."

"What's in Austin?" Jimmy's voice sounded in the doorway and Deb turned to find him looking as handsome as ever in jeans and a green T-shirt. "I was in town and I thought I'd stop by and see you," he explained when she gave him an I-thought-we-were-supposed-to-meet-later look. "About the wedding," he blurted when he caught Dolores' bifocals trained on him. "As the best man and maid of honor, we have duties." He grinned until the old woman blushed and went back to her column. "So what's in Austin?" he asked again as he walked up to her desk.

"Only the biggest awards ceremony in Texas and Deb, here, is a sure thing for Best Weekly."

"We've been nominated. That doesn't mean we're going to win."

"We're going to win," Wally informed him.

"Then we'll find out by mail because I can't go," Deb said, grabbing her purse and taking Jimmy's hand. "Subject closed."

"WHY DON'T YOU want to go?" Jimmy asked her later that night as they lay spoon fashion, their hearts still pounding, their bodies slick with sweat from their lovemaking.

"I already said." She stared at the lake just beyond the window. "I have to work."

"That's a lame excuse."

"You're a fine one to talk. You're up and out of here before daybreak, and all in the name of work."

"It's different for me. I've got people depending on me. My family."

"Wally and Paige and Dolores are like family to me." After a silent moment, she added, "Okay, Wally and Paige are like family. Dolores is more like a scary distant relative."

"You could still get away if you wanted to."

She shook her head. "I don't have anything to wear."

"Lame."

"I don't have a date."

He pulled her onto her back and leaned over her, his lips so close to hers, his smile a slash of white in the darkness. "I could always be your date."

"The ceremony's in two weeks and our business is finished in four days. You do the math."

"We could renegotiate."

The words sent a thrill through her that she quickly tamped down. "I've managed to keep tongues from wagging so far, but Dolores is a volcano about to blow. Not to mention, you and I on an actual date would tarnish your reputation."

"Maybe I don't care about my reputation."

She eyed him, wanting to believe him and at the same time hating herself for the strange urge. "And maybe I'm about to give birth to a litter of pigs," she finally said.

Before she knew what was happening, Jimmy ducked under the sheet. Large hands urged her thighs apart and she felt the exquisite probe of his fingers between her legs.

"What are you doing down there?"

"Looking for a litter of pigs." The sensation continued for several more delicious moments. His strong fingers touching and stroking and thrusting. "I hate to tell you this," he finally murmured, his voice a thrilling vibration against the tender inside of her thigh, "but I don't think you could fit one much less a litter." He slid up her body and settled between her open legs, his rock-hard erection nudging her slick opening. His eyes glittered in the moonlight, his smile warming the air between them. "But I do know something that will fit."

A smile played at her lips. "And what, pray tell, would that be?"

"This." He thrust his hard length inside her, stretching and filling. "Just what I thought," he growled when he'd sunk hilt-deep. "A perfect fit."

In more ways than one.

The thought struck her as she stared into his eyes and felt a connection unlike anything she'd ever felt before. They did more than touch physically. They talked. Shared. Connected.

She forced the crazy thoughts aside. So what if she and Jimmy could actually talk to each other? So what if she understood his pain over losing his father because she'd lost her granny Lily? So what if she knew the same guilt? So what if she understood why Jimmy was driving himself at the ranch?

Understanding didn't change who they were or what they wanted out of life. And he still wanted a nice little woman who looked good in a pair of overalls and knew her way around a barn—two things Deb had no intention of adding to her list of accomplishments. And she wanted her freedom.

Soon they would both go their separate ways. Jimmy would go about getting what he wanted and Deb would once again be single and free.

Unfortunately, the thought didn't hold near the appeal as it had the week before.

HE WAS plum crazy.

That was the only explanation for the fact that the more Jimmy touched Deb, the more he kissed her and slid deep inside, the more he wanted.

Crazy, all right.

While he managed to get himself up and out of bed every morning before the crack of dawn, it wasn't getting easier the way he'd expected. The way he'd hoped.

He stood beside the bed early Tuesday morning—a week and a half to the day he'd first gotten her into his bed—and stared down at her luscious body spread out on his cotton sheets.

Cotton, he reminded himself. While Deb was more the silk-sheets type, he'd given those up when he'd left Houston. Just as he was going to give her up come Sunday morning, after they spent their last night together.

He left the cabin and headed out to the small barn a few feet from the back porch where he'd left Emmaline; he'd started riding his horse to the cabin after finishing up at the ranch because it took less time and he was always anxious to get there.

He *had* to give her up. He told himself that as he saddled his horse and rode back to the ranch. He had to give her up and forget about their time together and start thinking about the future. About—

"Jimmy!"

The name rang out and scattered his thoughts the minute he walked into the kitchen. Actually, crept would have been a better word. Slowly and softly, and still he'd run smack-dab into his mother, who sat at the kitchen table, obviously waiting for him.

"Mornin', Ma." He dropped a kiss onto her cheek before turning to head back out the door. "I was just on my way out."

"Jimmy, I think—"

"I won't be home for lunch."

"But—"

"The wedding's tomorrow and I have to help Tack with a few last-minute things." His hand closed around the doorknob. He was almost home free...

"James Nathaniel Mission! You march back here and sit down right now. I want to talk to you."

"I've really got a lot of work—"

"Now, mister!"

Seconds later, he found himself seated across the kitchen table from his mother who was, as usual, fully dressed, her hair and makeup done as if she were ready for a night on the town rather than a day at the ranch.

She knew. She'd probably just come from an all-night prayer session and had her ear talked off. Deb said Dolores was a volcano, and she'd probably spewed all over his mother.

"Look, I know what you're going to say and you don't have to worry," he told her. "I have no interest in Deb Strickland. We're just friends."

"That's nice, dear. Now, listen. Mildred's daughter is just back from college, recently graduated, I might add. She's taking over Dr. Sumner's clinic and settling right here in town and I was thinking that you could show her around."

"Show her around?"

"Yes. Maybe even take her out to dinner and a little dancing." A secretive smile crossed her face. "Yes, definitely dancing."

Relief swept through him, short-lived when he realized what his mother was doing. "You're fixing me up?"

"You work too much. At the rate you're going, you'll never meet a nice girl and settle down." Her expression softened. "Do this for me, Jimmy. I've met her and she's wonderful. You'll enjoy yourself." Desperation laced each word and the truth crystallized.

His mother was trying to get him to date, to find a woman, to settle down, and all to reassure herself that he wasn't going to walk away again.

"Mom, I don't need to enjoy myself. I'm happy doing what I'm doing."

"I'm not saying you aren't. I just want you to do this for me. Please. I've never asked you for anything, but I'm asking now."

"I really don't..." His words trailed off as a vision of Deb pushed into his mind, but he quickly pushed it back out. His relationship with her was drawing to a close. They had tonight and then tomorrow night, after Annie and Tack's wedding. Then it was over.

When he'd mentioned renegotiating, she'd flat-out refused.

He didn't owe her any loyalty, but he did owe his mother.

"Okay."

A smile curved her lips. "Thank you. I'll let Mildred know and she'll tell Sarah you'll be calling." She produced a small piece of paper. "Call her, Jimmy," she said again.

"I will."

10

"THANKS AGAIN for letting me stay here tonight," Annie told Deb on Friday evening. "I really don't want Tack to see me before the wedding. It's tradition."

"Speaking of tradition." Deb reached for the sack of goodies she'd picked up at the store. "Tonight's your last night as a free woman and it's our duty to make the most of it."

"As in you helping me iron for my honeymoon?" Annie asked hopefully.

"As in getting wild and crazy. Kicking up our heels. Howling at the moon."

After two hours seated next to Jimmy at the rehearsal dinner—two long hours of feeling him next to her, all the while keeping her hands to herself because she didn't want to stir any gossip—she wanted to howl, all right. In frustration.

She needed a distraction in the worst way.

"I really do need to iron," Annie told her.

"You need to relax. To get your mind off the ironing and the cake and the flowers and—"

"Ohmigod! The cake. I forgot to tell Mrs. Wells to put little motorcycles on the groom's cake instead of the horses." Annie rushed to the phone and started dialing. "Tack loves motorcycles and the horse figurines look more like kangaroos."

"See?" Deb pointed to Annie's iron grip on the receiver. "You're wound much too tight."

"I just want everything to be—Mrs. Wells? This is Annie Divine. About the groom's cake..." She blurted out several instructions before sliding the receiver into place.

"Like I was saying," Deb went on. "You need to forget about everything." *She* needed to forget a certain handsome and tender cowboy.

Handsome she could have handled—his sexy grin, his sparkling eyes, his hunky body. It was the tender part she had trouble with. The way he held her so tightly after they made love each night, as if he didn't want to let her go.

As if.

"I need a distraction." At Annie's puzzled look, she quickly added, "I mean *we*. We need a distraction from the stress of the past few weeks, and you definitely need something to calm your nerves."

Annie drew in a deep, shaky breath. "Tomorrow's really the big day, isn't it?"

Deb nodded. "Which makes tonight your last night of freedom. Trust me, once you're married you won't get an opportunity to indulge yourself very often. First, you're too wrapped up in Tack, catering to him, doing for him. Then the kids come along and there goes anything remotely fun."

"Geez, you're really making me excited about tomorrow."

"You know what I mean. Marriage is about sharing yourself, about sacrifice." About following instructions and playing the good little spouse. "But this..." Deb indicated the bag she'd placed on the counter. "This is about indulging yourself."

"But I really have to be up early in the morning and I still have a million things—"

"You have to do this," Deb cut in. "We have to do this. It's tradition. Isn't Tack out with the guys right now?"

"Actually, he's in. They're barbecuing at the ranch, playing darts, watching some football—typical guy stuff."

"Which is why we should do some typical girl stuff. It's your duty to really live it up, and it's my duty as maid of honor to see that you do. Come on, Annie. It'll be fun."

Annie peeked inside the bag and a smile curved her lips. "Well, it *is* tradition."

"Damn straight it is," Deb said as she pulled out a gallon of Chocolate Ecstasy, followed by a bottle of hot fudge sauce, some caramel and a container of whipped cream. "Besides, I already invited the rest of the gang. You have your entire life to spend with Tack, but tonight it's just girls, goodies and some major gabbing."

She inhaled, letting the sweet aroma of chocolate decadence fill her nostrils. Her stomach grumbled in anticipation, a different sort of need taking control.

Mission accomplished.

"AND SHE TOLD EVERYBODY that Jessica had not one, but two boob jobs," Dolores said.

"I'd ask for my money back," Deb said around a mouthful of her second hot fudge sundae. "She looks as flat as before."

"That's because she really didn't have a boob job done, much less two. She had that stuff injected into her lips instead."

"Collagen," Paige piped up, licking hot fudge from her spoon.

"My lips hurt just thinking about that," Annie said before shoveling in a spoon of whipped cream.

"The lengths women go to to please a man." Wally snorted. "Haven't you women figured out that all you have to do is breathe, and we're there?"

"Now I know why you don't have a girlfriend," Deb told him.

"I don't want to tie myself down."

"Speaking of being tied down," Dolores rushed on. "Remember Wilma Gentry and that long 'vacation' she took last year?"

"The cruise?" Annie asked.

"I heard it was a camping trip," Wally piped in.

"Gambling excursion to Vegas," Deb added.

"Dominatrix convention," Dolores told them. "I heard it from my sister's best friend's mother who saw Wilma buying this dog collar at the Piggly Wiggly and—"

Rrrring!

"—she doesn't even own a dog!"

"Maybe it was for her neighbor's dog."

"Or maybe it was for her cat."

"Or maybe she was buying it for her friend."

"My thoughts exactly," Dolores said, "but then Travis Windburn is out walking his dog late at night and sees her in the window wearing a—"

Rrrring!

"Hold it." Deb held up a hand. "Don't say another word until I get back. I have to hear this." She pushed to her feet and headed toward the kitchen.

"Tell us something else while she's gone," Paige said excitedly.

"Yeah, something juicy," Annie added.

"Well, I heard from Maureen Rodgers, she's the head cashier, that Mildred Cook's daughter was buying Ho-Ho's and just happened to mention that she was going to dinner with one hunky Jimmy Mission next Friday night—"

"What?" Deb stopped in the kitchen doorway and whirled. "He's *what?*"

"Taking her to dinner. I don't know where, but there's always the meat loaf special at the diner. Of course, Jimmy's liable to spring for the full monty and take her to one of those fancy steak houses out on the Interstate. Sarah's a hot commodity for the ranchers around these parts... Dear, are you all right?" At Deb's silence, Dolores rushed on, "You swore to me that you two weren't sweet on each other. You said—"

"We're not," Deb blurted. "Did you say Jimmy? I thought you said Timmy. Timmy Milton. Boy, is that man a cutie," she mumbled before turning and stumbling into the kitchen.

Jimmy?

Mildred's daughter?

Friday night?

"Hello?" she mumbled when she finally got to the ringing phone, her brain still trying to digest the news.

Jimmy and Sarah. Sarah and Jimmy. Jimmy—

"Hey, there, Slick."

As if her frantic thoughts had conjured him, his voice poured over the line like warm chocolate fudge over ice cream and her heart stalled, only to pound forward.

"Jimmy," she choked out, doing her best to swallow past the sudden lump in her throat.

"The one and only. Listen, I was thinking..." His words faded as a round of laughter exploded in the living room. "What's going on over there?"

"Annie's staying the night."

"I know, which is why I thought we could meet at my... What's all that noise?"

"A bachelorette party."

"We're out of ice cream!" Wally called from the living room.

"I'll bring some out in a minute," she called back. "So did you go to Tack's bachelor barbecue?"

"For a little while."

"Did Sarah Cook jump out of the cake?"

"We didn't have cake. It was a barbecue." His voice took on a strange note. "Are you okay? You sound funny."

More like stunned. Angry. Hurt. "I'm fine," she blurted. "So is it over?"

"I left early. I thought we could—"

"And whipped cream!" Wally's voice rang out.

"Who was that?"

"Just somebody asking for more whipped cream," Deb told him. "You thought we could what?"

"Well, I thought—"

"And hot fudge! Don't forget the hot fudge!"

"Sure thing," she called. "So?" she prodded Jimmy.

"That's a guy's voice," he said, an edge of steel underlying the statement.

"Yeah."

"What's a guy doing at your place asking for ice cream and whipped cream?"

"Don't forget the hot fudge," she added. "I really have to go. I'm missing the fun." She hung up before she did something stupid like scream at him. Or worse, cry.

She blinked her eyes frantically. She was not crying. And she certainly wasn't crying over Jimmy or that he was taking Mildred Cook's daughter—her single, homely, horse-loving daughter—to dinner less than one week after their 'business arrangement' came to an end.

A date. He was going on a date.

As if he'd never bought her that canister of coffee or held her or made love to her with an intensity that went far beyond lust.

As if Deb Strickland were just any woman.

While she wasn't next in line for Queen of the Cow Patties like most of the other women in hot pursuit of studly Jimmy Mission, she wasn't chopped liver either. She had a lot to offer a marriage-minded man. She was fairly attractive, smart, successful, nice—on most occasions when Jimmy wasn't yanking her chain—and she could sew.

While the *last* thing she wanted was to be Jimmy's wife—any man's wife—it was the principle of the thing that mattered. That, and the fact that Jimmy Mission felt more for her than passing interest.

She wasn't fool enough to think he'd fallen in love with her, any more than she was fool enough to fall in love with him. Love was highly overrated and Deb would not, could not, fall in love with Jimmy Mission.

But care about him... Yes, she *did* care about him. And he cared about her.

She told herself that, yet doubt plagued her for the

next hour as she made more hot fudge sundaes and did her best to concentrate on Dolores and all the juicy gossip.

"Are you okay?" Annie asked once when they were alone in the kitchen together.

"I'm just a little preoccupied."

"You and Jimmy still haggling over the money you owe him?"

"No, we've come to an agreement about that." That's why she was in this quandary. Because they'd made an agreement and spent the past two weeks together and now he was taking someone else on a date as if he didn't even care.

Not that it mattered if he did or didn't. She was still saying *adios* and sending him off into the sunset. It didn't matter....

It did. For some weird insane reason that she couldn't name, she wanted him to feel more for her than he felt for the other women in his fan club. She wanted to matter to him. For him to remember her. To never forget.

"I'm glad," Annie went on. "I told you all you had to do was talk to him. He's a nice guy."

"Just my luck," Deb grumbled as she walked out onto the back porch to stuff a bag into the trash can. Jimmy *was* a nice guy, and handsome and charming and sweet, which was why she was having all these ridiculous feelings for him. Meanwhile, he was lining up dates.

Maybe he really didn't feel anymore for her than he felt for anyone else—

"Where is he?" The voice, low and deep and desperate, came from behind her a split second before an arm slid around her waist and pulled her back up against a familiar male body.

"Jimmy," she breathed. Her heart started beating again as relief flooded through her, a feeling that quickly faded when the smell of warm male and aftershave flared her nostrils and made her blood pump faster.

"Come on. Where?"

"Who?"

"The guy with the whipped cream and cherries. Who else?"

"Inside."

He walked past her into the kitchen and ducked his head into the living room for a quick look. "That's Wally," he said when the kitchen door had swung shut.

"Yeah."

He gave her a murderous glare and something warm unfurled inside her. "I thought you had a guy here."

"I *do* have a guy here. Not that I've personally checked, but rumor has it that Wally's fully equipped and—"

"You know what I mean. You let me think you were entertaining."

She couldn't help the smile that played at her lips. "If I didn't know better, I'd say you were jealous."

The word seemed to trigger something and his expression eased, as if he'd just realized that he was standing in her kitchen at midnight, demanding to know who she had in her living room. "I'm interested, yes," he drawled. "I had plans for you tonight."

She leaned up and kissed his cheek. "Sorry, but

Annie's spending the night, her last as a free woman, and I promised her we'd do facials and other girl stuff."

His fingertip caught a smear of chocolate sauce at the corner of her mouth and heat bolted through her. "A facial?"

"Facials are for later. We're doing the rejuvenating hot fudge sundae right now. It stimulates the taste buds and frees the spirit. You know what they say about chocolate—it's one of the best aphrodisiacs. I bet if a girl ate enough of these, even Wally would start to look good." She meant to get a rise out of him, and for about an eighth of a second, she thought she saw anger flicker in his green eyes. But then it was gone, fading into an easy smile and a teasing grin.

"Save some for tomorrow night, then." He dropped a kiss onto her nose and walked out the back door.

Okay, so it wasn't exactly the declaration of devotion she'd been hoping for, but everyone knew that actions spoke louder than words. He'd burst into her house in the middle of the night because he'd thought she had a man inside. He *did* care about her.

He just wouldn't admit it. Yet.

HE WAS NOT JEALOUS.

Jimmy sat outside in his pickup truck, watched Deb's silhouette move in front of a living-room window, and barely ignored the urge to storm inside and hoist her over his shoulder.

Before he could do any more damage, he gunned the engine and shoved the gearshift into reverse. A few seconds later, he was peeling down the highway, heading back toward his cabin.

He knew what had him so worked up. So nervous and anxious and angry. Not because Deb had led him on a wild-goose chase, but because he'd come running at nothing more than the hint of a man at her place. He'd climbed into his pickup and hauled ass into town, his heart pumping, anger and fear clawing at his gut because Deb Strickland was his.

Yep, he was crazy, all right. Certi-goddamn-fiable.

Deb Strickland in no way belonged to him. It was simply the Texas heat frying his brain and impairing his judgment and making him think all sorts of possessive thoughts.

He flipped the air conditioner on high and rolled the windows up. There. No more frying or impairing or thinking possessive thoughts. *No more.* His relationship with Deb was about sex in the here and now, not waking up together every morning of every tomorrow.

Jimmy needed a different sort of woman for that—*need* being the key word. *Need* cut through all the frivolous stuff and went straight to the heart of the matter. It was all about basic survival, about what a man *had* to have to make it in his life. His *new* life. The one he was building here in Inspiration.

For Jimmy, basic survival involved continuing his father's legacy and taking care of what was really *his*—the land and the cattle—and for that he needed a forever kind of woman, not the queen of fun.

No matter how much he wanted her.

He knew what he'd *also* wooded inc. So ahead...
and *gas* me awry. Neither one Did her let ...
to a *wild gace* daze. But because *he* *favours* her
was a *wolf* ling *in a* *chance* boast of *a time*. They
plans, *he'd* *charted* *in* *his power* and *hurled* as
the *moor* *of one's* *primary* *ange* *the* *far* *young*
At *last* *in* *be* *true* *loss*, *sweet* *land* *was* *his*
care. He *was* *slow* *all* *in* *here* *love* *you* *with*

11

SHE WAS NOT going to cry.

Deb told herself that Saturday afternoon as she helped Annie into her gown. But the moment she slid the final button of the dress into place and handed her friend the bouquet, the tears started.

"Oh, no. You're crying," Annie said.

"I've just got something in my eye," Deb said, snatching up her own bouquet and heading outside to take her place at the entrance to the huge white tent that had been set up at the Big B Ranch, Tack Brandon's place and now officially Annie's, too. Rows of white chairs filled the structure, the center aisle anchored on either side with rows of tulle and flowers.

"I hate this monkey suit," Wally said after he'd finished escorting Pastor Marley's wife to her seat. "Remind me never to agree to be an usher again—" The words stopped as his gaze fixed on hers. "Well, I'll be damned. You're crying."

"In your dreams. I stabbed my eye with the mascara wand." She blinked frantically and tugged at the floor-length pastel colored maid of honor's dress she wore.

"Don't give me that. You can do that makeup stuff blindfolded." He smirked. "You're crying all right."

"Who's crying?" Paige rushed up, looking like a

walking flower bed with an ankle-length dress covered with daisies and marigolds.

"Deb," Wally said. "I told you she was an Eskimo pie."

"You're both fired," Deb snapped as she rushed over to the photographer and barked a few last-minute orders on Annie's behalf.

Blink, she told herself as she started her trek down the aisle. Five steps and she managed to gather her composure—until her gaze hooked on Jimmy standing at the end beside Tack and Pastor Marley.

He was the best man.

The *only* man.

The thought struck her along with a crystal clear vision of him dressed just as he was now, waiting at the end of the aisle as she floated toward him wearing a wedding gown.

It wasn't so much the image that stopped her cold, her heels sticking to the red carpet for a long moment. It was the feeling that pulsed through her—a culmination of warmth and excitement and anticipation.

At being Jimmy Mission's bride?

Before she could ponder the thought, the flower girl bumped into her and spurred her into action. Deb picked up her steps, rushing forward, all the while desperate to calm her pounding heart and ignore the man whose gaze followed her for the remainder of the ceremony.

"Here," Jimmy handed her a handkerchief after the vows were said and Annie and Tack had taken their victory walk up the aisle. Then he took her arm and guided her back along the same carpet-lined path.

"I'm crying," she snapped at his knowing gaze. "So what?"

"So, nothing." He didn't press the matter or smile that damnable smile or look smug because she was being such a baby. He simply squeezed her hand reassuringly and steered her through the crowd, outside to a sprawling oak tree where she could blow her nose in private.

"I don't usually cry, but there's been a high pollen count in the air," she told him.

"Heard about that myself."

She sniffled. "Off the charts."

"Annie made a real pretty bride, didn't she?"

"Beautiful." Another sniffle and she wiped at a lone tear before handing Jimmy back his handkerchief. "Thanks."

"You keep it." His hand closed around hers for a long, heart-pounding second. "They're cutting the cake in a few minutes and I wouldn't want that high pollen count to keep you from getting a good look."

She couldn't help herself. She smiled. "Thanks."

"My pleasure."

Actually, it was hers. He was touching her, just the slight pressure of his fingers surrounding hers, and her nerves were buzzing like a swarm of excited children on the Fourth of July. And his gaze, so serious and intense and concerned.... Yes, *concern* glimmered hot and bright, and warmth unfurled inside her.

Then he did something that ruined everything.

He smiled that charming smile and winked, and she was back to being just any woman.

"We're missing the pictures," she snapped, marching around him and heading back toward the tent.

"Wait up." He was right on her heels. "What's eating you?"

"Nothing."

"Then why are you stomping away like an angry bull?"

She whirled on him. "Do you care? Do you *really* care?"

A strange expression passed over his face before his eyes crinkled and a grin curved his lips. "Sure I do. Tell me what's bothering you, and I'll see what I can do to set things right."

Any woman.

"You," she tapped him in the chest with a pink manicured nail. "You're bothering me." And then she marched past him toward the reception area before she did something really scandalous like strangle Jimmy Mission on the spot.

As tempting as the idea was, she needed him alive and well if she intended to carry out her plan and force him to admit that he did feel more for her than just lust.

And if he didn't admit it?

Deb pushed the thought aside. The night was young and they didn't call her shameless for nothing.

THE WOMAN was driving him to drink.

Jimmy finished off the last of his second beer and reached for number three as he watched Deb two-step around the dance floor with one of Tack's ranch hands. Even dressed in a mint-green bridesmaid's dress that was too frilly for his simple tastes, she looked good enough to eat. With every turn, the skirt flew up, revealing long, slender legs. With every dip, the bodice of her dress shifted and he glimpsed the soft swells of her breasts. A thin line of perspiration dotted her forehead, making her face glow. Her lips were full and red and parted in a smile—

Hell's bells, she was *smiling* at that two-bit cowboy.

Jimmy latched onto beer number four as the song played down and Deb traded Tack's ranch hand and the two-step for one of Jimmy's own men and a lively polka.

She twirled and swayed and smiled— Hell's bells, there she was smiling again. And winking. Holy God, she was actually *winking* at one of his men.

Beer number five arrived just as Pastor Marley's nephew cut in for a waltz. Jimmy's hands tightened on the bottle of Bud and he fought back the urge to rush over, pull Deb into his arms and make her smile and wink at him. An urge he managed to resist until one of Tack's racing buddies approached her. When the good-looking man took her in his arms for a slow country swing, Jimmy forgot all about his beer.

"Are you through making a fool of yourself?" he demanded as he met her coming off the dance floor. She was breathless and laughing and the sight made him all the more angry.

Her head tilted back and she met his glare, a smile curving her full lips. "Actually, I was just getting started."

"In case you've forgotten, we came here together."

"So?"

"So...we *came* together, and we're damn sure leaving together."

"Not right now we aren't. I'm in the mood to dance."

"Fine." He took her hand and pulled her up

against him. "I'm cutting in, buddy," he told her stunned partner.

"What are you doing?" she asked as he steered her out onto the dance floor.

"You're in the mood to dance, so let's dance."

"Maybe I don't want to dance with you." Or anyone for that matter. As accustomed as Deb was to three-inch heels, the four-and-half-inch babies she'd donned for the wedding were taking their toll, especially after she'd spent the past half hour trying to get Jimmy's attention, to get under his skin and up his body temperature. "Maybe I'd rather dance with somebody else."

He stared her down, a dozen emotions fighting in his gaze and she worried that his control would win, that he would smile that charming smile and whisper in his sweet-as-warm-honey drawl, "Be my guest."

"Dammit, Slick," he growled, sliding a possessive arm around her waist and pulling her closer. "You really piss me off." The words echoed through her head and satisfaction welled inside her.

"Thank you, Jimmy." She pressed a kiss to the tanned column of his throat before glancing up, her gaze meeting his.

He stared at her as if she'd donned a No Beef cap and declared herself a vegetarian. "You are the most infuriating woman I've ever had the misfortune to meet."

"I know." And then there were no more words as he pulled her closer and she nestled her head in the curve of his neck. The rest of the world faded and they started to dance.

DEB HAD WON the battle, but not the war, she realized the next morning when she rolled over after a night of

Jimmy's usual slow and thorough lovemaking to find the bed next to her warm, but empty. She heard him moving around in the kitchen—the creak of the chair as he yanked on his boots, the slide of change as he loaded his pockets, the clink of a coffee cup as he finished his last swallow. He was leaving. It was still dark, still a half hour shy of sunrise, and Jimmy was heading out to work, to his land and his cattle and his duty, despite last night.

Admiration crept through her, along with a surge of anxiety. This was it. Their last few moments together. Once the sun rose, the night would be officially over, their business concluded. It was now or never. Otherwise, she would never really know that she'd meant more to him, that she'd been anything other than a passing interest, a casual fling, a business arrangement. She wanted to have been more than his lover.

Not his love, of course. Jimmy Mission had made it clear that he wasn't falling in love with her. She wasn't his type, and Lord knew he wasn't hers. She simply wanted to know that after today, he would at least think about her every now and then. Remember her. She wanted, *needed* a place in Jimmy Mission's memory since she couldn't, *wouldn't* claim a place in his heart.

Now or never.

JIMMY HAD JUST retrieved a blanket from the tack room and walked back to Emmaline's stall, when the barn door creaked open. For a split second, a thrill went through him before it faded in a wave of reality because it couldn't be Deb. No way would she be up at this ungodly—

The thought jolted to a halt when he caught sight of her—her long, dark hair tousled, her face soft and flushed from sleep, her lips swollen from a night of lovemaking. She wore only his white tuxedo shirt and an old, worn pair of his boots. The shirt stopped midthigh, revealing long, sexy-as-hell legs. Despite that the previous night marked their *last* night together and Jimmy's appetite should have long ago been sated, he felt a stir in his groin.

It was followed by a quick jolt of unease as she walked into the barn. The tuxedo shirt, unbuttoned to reveal the swell of her luscious breasts, tugged and pulled and teased him with each step. Her tattoo winked at him with every breath she took.

Work, he told himself, forcing his gaze away, determined to get the blasted saddle on Emmaline and get back to the ranch before his crew awoke. He had to set an example—not to mention he had a full day ahead with cows to brand and fences to mend. A rancher was coming in from Midland this afternoon to look over Valentino as a breeding prospect. Then there was his mother. He'd promised her a dance last night, and he'd forgotten all about it.

Hell, he'd forgotten everything except Deb.

He felt her gaze and every nerve in his body snapped to attention. He frowned. He was in the homestretch. No more wanting what he couldn't have. No more Deb.

As relieved as the thought should have made him, the only thing he felt at that moment was desperation.

To get out of here, he reminded himself. He was desperate for a quick exit. End of story.

"What are you doing out here?" he asked gruffly.

"Same as you." Boots crunched as she neared the stall. "I thought I'd take a ride."

The words drew his gaze and he found her standing on the opposite side of the stall. "I hate to break it to you, Slick, but you can't ride."

"Wanna bet?" Her eyes glittered. Her full lips curved into a half smile that did funny things to his heartbeat. "For your information, I can set a saddle as good as you." As if to prove her point, she gripped the saddlehorn of the saddle he'd draped over the stall wall, swung a sexy leg over and mounted up. "See?"

He could see all right. A delicious display of thigh and hip that stalled the air in his lungs. "That saddle is not exactly attached to five hundred pounds of living, breathing horseflesh."

"Then I'm definitely in for a smooth ride." She shifted in her seat as if demonstrating. "Not too hard or too bumpy. Just a little rocking back and forth, this way and that...." She closed her eyes and started to move, to and fro, side to side. "Mmm... Now I know why you cowboys spend so much time in the saddle."

"I don't think it's the same for us cowboys. Different parts."

Her eyes opened then and her passion-filled blue eyes met his. "I know."

They stared at each other for several fast furious heartbeats, before Jimmy found the courage to turn away, to put his mind on his horse and the fact that he'd hoisted the blanket on unevenly and the damned thing had slipped off the other side. "I really don't have time for this. I'm going to have to ride hard as it is."

"Mmm... Now there's an idea."

Her words rang in his ears, her meaning obvious and he shook his head. Nah. He was reading her wrong. She didn't mean... She couldn't mean...

He chanced a glance out of the corner of his eye and saw her—her head thrown back, eyes closed, lips parted as she arched her breasts and rocked her lower body. It was a sight he was all too familiar with after the past couple of weeks with her.

A sight that shouldn't affect him. After two weeks together, she was out of his system. His head was on straight, his mind back on business, his goals crystal clear in front of him.

He forced his attention back to the horse and retrieved the fallen blanket. Hoisting the thing onto the animal's back, he was in the process of straightening it when a soft, familiar sigh quivered in the air.

The sound sent a bolt of need through him, along with a fierce wave of possessiveness that burned away reason and made him forget everything but reckless desire and the need to claim what was his. To hell with the damned blanket. He closed the distance between them in two quick steps.

A man could only take so much and this woman— correction, *any* woman—heating up the seat of his saddle would have been too much for the average Joe to take.

At the first touch of his fingertips on her thigh, her eyes fluttered open.

She stared down at him, her eyes bright and feverish and knowing. "I thought you were in a hurry."

"I am. I'm in a hurry to find out what you're wearing under that shirt." He reached across her lap and urged her other leg over the saddle until she sat sideways, facing him, her lap level with his shoulders.

"Nothing," he murmured as he shoved the shirt up and spread her legs wide, wedging his shoulders between her knees. "Ah, baby, you're so beautiful." Her slick folds were pink and swollen after her recent activities on his saddle, and he knew she was close. "So wet." He touched her, trailed a fingertip over the hot, moist flesh and relished the moan that vibrated from her lips.

There were no more words after that. None of his usual teasing. He didn't even give her his trademark grin. He simply hooked her booted ankles over his shoulders, tilted her body a fraction just to give him better access, dipped his head and tasted her sweetness.

She cried out at the first lap of his tongue and threaded her fingers through his hair to hold him close. But he wasn't going anywhere. This was her ride and Jimmy intended to make it the wildest, most memorable of her life.

He devoured her, licking and sucking and nibbling, pushing her higher and higher, and oddly enough, climbing right along with her. He took his own pleasure by pleasuring her and when she screamed his name and came apart in his arms, the feelings that rushed through him—the triumph and the satisfaction and the warmth—felt as good as any orgasm he'd ever had.

Chemistry, a voice whispered. They were simply good together. That explained her effect on him.

He wanted to think so. He *needed* to think it. But it

was more, he admitted to himself as he stared up into her flushed face and tenderness welled up inside him. More than the physical.

As crazy as it was, he didn't just want to hoist her over his shoulder, take her back to the cabin and drive deep, deep inside her hot delicious body until he reached his own climax.

He wanted to curl up with her afterward, talk to her, laugh with her, hold her when she got that soft, misty-eyed look, and argue with her just to see the sparks flare in her eyes.

Despite the responsibilities that waited for him, he wanted to forget about the rest of the world beyond the cabin walls. It was a feeling that had nothing to do with chemistry and the fact that he'd always had a thing for bold and beautiful women, and everything to do with her smile and her sass and her attitude and *her*.

Need gripped him, fierce and demanding and intense. He gathered her in his arms and started for the cabin.

"What about work?" she murmured against his neck.

"It'll wait."

THE MINUTE Jimmy pressed her down on the bed, Deb knew something had changed. There was an urgency, a fierceness about him that she'd never seen before. Tension held his body tight, every muscle taut. His hands felt strong and purposeful and desperate as he ripped off his clothes, spread her legs wide and slid home in one fierce thrust.

"You are the damnedest woman," he growled,

resting his forehead against hers for several fast, furious heartbeats, "*My* woman."

She didn't expect the declaration anymore than the determination that glittered in his eyes as he stared down at her, into her. And she certainly didn't anticipate the pure joy that rushed through her.

Before she could dwell on the feeling, large hands gripped her buttocks and tilted. He slid a fraction deeper and all rational thought fled.

The next few moments passed in a frenzy of need as Jimmy pumped into her over and over, as if his life depended on every deep, penetrating thrust. His mouth ate at hers, and his touch was greedy and hungry, as if he could no longer control his need for her. As if he'd stopped trying. They joined together on a basic, primitive level unlike anything she'd ever experienced before, and as she stared up into his face, at his fierce, wild expression, she knew she'd driven him over the edge.

For the first time, Jimmy Mission had lost his precious control.

The realization sent a thrill coursing through her, followed by warning bells. But before she could worry over what the change meant, he slid his hand between them and touched her where they joined, and she went wild with him.

Seconds later, she screamed his name for the second time that morning as her climax slammed into her and she shattered in his arms. Another fierce, pounding thrust, and Jimmy followed her into oblivion, her name bursting from his lips as he spilled himself deep inside.

"I love you," he groaned as he collapsed atop her,

his arms solid and warm, his body pressing her into the mattress.

I love you. The words echoed through her head and sent a swell of happiness through her for a full moment before Deb remembered the last thing, the *very* last thing she wanted from Jimmy Mission was his love.

Love? He couldn't... He wouldn't... *No!* This wasn't happening. Not him and her and *love.*

"I—I have to go." She scrambled from the bed, her heart pounding furiously as she snatched up her clothes in record time. And then Deb did what any freedom-loving woman would do with a hunky, naked, sexy cowboy who loved her right at her fingertips.

She ran for her life.

12

Jimmy sat on the side of the bed and listened to the rev of Deb's Miata, the squeal of tires as she shoved it into reverse, and barely resisted the urge to go after her.

Hell, he would have except he had no clue what to say. He'd said more than enough already. More than she wanted to hear.

A wave of regret rolled through him and he damned himself for being so stupid, for letting things get so out of hand, for letting her distract him, for letting his own damned emotions get the best of him. Christ, he hadn't even worn a condom. Unfortunately, the realization didn't bother him near as much as it should have.

He'd lost it.

That was the only explanation for what he'd done and said and *felt*. Deb Strickland was not the type of woman Jimmy meant to spend the rest of his life with. He needed a woman who could work side-by-side with him. A woman who knew how to cook and clean and ride.

The last thought sent a very vivid image through his head of a beautiful brunette poised atop his saddle....

Okay, so he'd give her the riding part, but otherwise, she had none of the qualities he wanted in a wife. None of the qualities he needed to keep things going. His mother and father had built the ranch together, and Jimmy needed an equal partner to help him do the same. A self-reliant girl who could drive a tractor and doctor a sick horse. A good, God-fearing, land-loving, salt-of-the-earth type just like his mother. A woman who wasn't afraid to sacrifice, and Deb had already made it clear that she wasn't a martyr.

She wouldn't last a week out at the Mission Ranch, miles from Sonia's Nail Salon and the beauty shop and the cosmetic section at the Piggly Wiggly. Not to mention, she'd never make it more than two steps from the back porch of the ranch house—*his* house, he reminded himself, though the cabin felt more like home—without sinking at least a few inches in those fancy high heels of hers.

No, she wasn't his type at all and he should chalk this morning up to the heat of the moment and get on about the business of finding a real wife. Deb was not the sort of woman Jimmy would even mention to his mother, much less take home as the future Lady Mission.

His poor mother was worried enough that her oldest son would leave and she'd be left to fend for herself. She hardly slept at night anymore. When he crept in just before daybreak, she was always up, fully dressed, as if she'd been too wound up to sleep. Too worried. As if she knew her son was keeping company with the most citified woman in town and she feared losing him to the lure of the bright lights the way she had so many years ago.

He couldn't, wouldn't desert her again when she needed him most, when the ranch needed him, and so it was best for him to just put his feelings aside, let Deb go and do the right thing.

That's what his father would have wanted. What Jimmy meant to do.

As of this moment, Deb was out of the picture. Off-limits. Completely out of his realm of consideration. And he *wasn't* mentioning her to his mother.

"MA? I REALLY NEED to talk to you." Jimmy rapped on his mother's bedroom door a short while later. "Ma?" He knocked, the door swinging open beneath the weight of his knuckles. "You see, there's this woman and she..." His words trailed off as he drank in the empty room. A light burned on the nightstand, revealing the still made bed, the pillows fluffed and untouched.

He turned and headed back down the hall toward the kitchen, guilt dogging his every step. Hell's bells, she'd probably spent the night pacing, drinking coffee, or—

Dancing? The thought struck him as he rounded the corner and spotted his mother creeping in the front door, fully dressed, a pair of high heels dangling from her hands and an I Was Born To Boogie button pinned to one of her best Sunday dresses.

He blinked, but she didn't disappear. She hunched over, trying to shut the door as silently as possible, and all of a sudden things fell into place—why his mother seemed to be avoiding him most of the time, why she looked so guilty, why she was always up and fully dressed before the crack of dawn.

He frowned as the door gave a soft *click* and his mother turned.

"Morning, Ma."

"Good morning, Jim—" The name stalled as her head jerked around and her eyes collided with his. "Jimmy," she said nervously. "My, my, you're up early this morning."

"And you're up sort of late."

A nervous grin creased her face as she shoved the heels behind her back. "I—I was just... That is, I thought I'd get an early start...." She licked her lips. "The weatherman says it's going to be such a perfect day that..." Her sentence trailed off as she seemed to come to a decision. "What am I doing? I don't have to make excuses. I'm the mother." She squared her shoulders and faced him. "I was out all night."

"Dancing?"

"How did you..." Her question trailed off as her gaze followed Jimmy's and she slapped a hand over her button. "A little souvenir. Red wanted to buy T-shirts, but those are so expensive and these buttons were really kind of cute and—"

"Red?" he cut in, his thoughts stalling on the name.

"Red Bailey. He's my dancing partner." She seemed to search for her courage. "Actually, he's more."

Red Bailey. The name echoed in his head and a picture rushed at Jimmy, of his mom dancing with Red at Annie's wedding last night.

All night.

His *mother.* The same woman who headed the church auxiliary and hosted the weekly prayer meeting and made it her business to be in bed at sunset just so she could get up at sunrise to feed her chickens.

"We went to a little place over in the next county,"

she was explaining, "that has all-night dancing after the reception and I guess we forgot the time."

There were a dozen questions he wanted to ask, but the only thing that sprang to his lips was a stunned, "I never knew you danced."

"I didn't. Your father never liked to. But then he passed away and I was bored and Nell suggested these dance classes. I refused at first, but then I said, What the hey? See, when your father died, I promised myself I wouldn't waste my life worrying over this place, so I started these dance classes. That's where I met Red. He's such a nice man, and boy, can he move."

"*Red?*" Jimmy said again, still trying to digest the information. His mother dancing with Red Bailey. His mother out all night with the man. "Red Bailey, the bronc rider?"

"The oldest bronc rider still on the circuit. Speaking of which, once we're married, I'll be going with him on the road—"

"Married?"

She nodded and a smile as bright as the Texas sun split her face. "Red asked me to marry him last night. He slid the ring on to my finger just as Annie and Tack exchanged rings. Isn't that romantic? We haven't set a date, but I already know I want Pastor Marley to perform the ceremony, and I want Nell as a bridesmaid, and I was thinking that maybe we could get the same woman who made Annie's wedding cake to—"

"Could we back up a little?" Jimmy cut in. "You and Red are getting *married?*"

She nodded.

"*You* and *Red?*"

Another nod.

"You're getting married and leaving the ranch? *This* ranch?" She nodded again. "Then what was all that stuff about Sarah Cook?"

"What about her, dear?"

"You fixed me up with her so that I'd settle down and stay right here with you and the ranch."

"No, I didn't. I fixed you up with her because she's single and she can dance a mean polka. You've been working so hard around here. Why, you haven't even been coming home at night to sleep. That's no way for a young man to live. You need to have some fun once in a while. You need to date."

He shook his head in amazement as the truth crystallized. "All this time, I thought you were afraid I'd leave again. I thought that you were afraid I'd desert you and leave you to run this place all by yourself. I thought you were lonely."

"I was. That's why I started taking dance lessons." A knowing look crept into her eyes as she touched his face. "Dear, you could leave tomorrow and I would surely miss you, but I would never think that you deserted me. You have your own life to live. I understand that. So did your father. That's why he never said a word when you left for the marines, or when you settled in Houston."

"He should have. I would have come home."

"Because he asked you to, not because you wanted to. Your father wanted you here, but only if it's where you wanted to be."

"But I should have been here when he passed away. I should have been right beside him. I could have gotten him to a doctor and—" The words stalled as she placed a fingertip to his lips.

"It was his time, Jimmy. We all have one. One day, mine will come and it won't matter if you're standing next to me or a thousand miles away. Your father is gone and you can't bring him back. You didn't cause his death anymore than you could have prevented it. He was old and stubborn and he knew better than to go out alone to fix that fence in the middle of the danged night. But that was his way. This place meant everything to him. He worked so hard—"

"—for us," Jimmy cut in. "For me and Jack, and how did I pay him back? By letting him die alone."

"You stop that right now, James Nathaniel Mission," his mother's expression grew stern. "Your father worked hard to build this place up for his boys, true enough, but first and foremost, he did it for himself. It was his own dream. He'd always wanted to have his own land and run his own cattle. From the first moment I met him, that's all he ever talked about. He was from the poorest family in Inspiration, but that didn't stop him from aspiring to better things. He was always dreaming about how he was going to make something of himself and be this big-shot rancher. The minute we tied the knot, he took his entire savings and bought five acres, and he started to build. The years wore on, and he kept building, always wanting more. For his family, but also for himself, to see his own dream realized." Sadness crept into her eyes. "At first, he didn't have time to relax. But later, when the place grew and he hired more hands and the time was there, he didn't want to relax. He couldn't. I think he got so used to driving himself, that he forgot how to slow down. Doc Sumners warned him about overdoing it. Take up bingo, the doc said. Play dominoes or cards or Monopoly. Do something that'll keep you off your feet and give your heart a rest. But your father was deaf when it came to anything that didn't involve the daily running of this ranch."

Jimmy frowned, his emotions raging as he remembered so many phone calls with his father and not one mention of any sort of heart condition. "Let me get this straight. The doctor warned Dad about a heart attack, and he didn't listen?"

"Several times. Your father used to have occasional chest pains, usually after a stressful day doing something or other. Why, he nearly collapsed after a branding session spring before last."

"But why didn't he *say* something? Why didn't you? I would have come home sooner. I would have—"

"—rushed back here out of that same sense of pigheaded duty that kept your father working twenty-hour days," she cut in. "You're a good son, Jimmy." A soft smile touched her face. "You always were. Jack would always be off getting himself into trouble." She shook her head. "Not you. You were always so mature and responsible when you were a boy. But you're all grown up now and your duty isn't to this place. Or me."

"But—"

"It's to yourself." She tapped his chest. "To what's inside here. Your father lived his life and now it's your turn. Just because you were raised on a ranch doesn't mean it's your destiny. Your father lived his dream, and you deserve to live yours." She smoothed a lock of hair away from his forehead and a desperate expression crept over her face. "Don't make the same mistakes he made, Jimmy. While he loved this ranch, he loved you and Jack even more. If this spread is what you want, what you *really* want, fine, but don't let it consume you."

Sounds to me like it isn't the ranching you love so much as that it reminds you of your dad.

Deb's words echoed in his head and he finally admitted to himself what he'd known all along. She was right. It wasn't the ranching itself he loved. It was the memories. The ranch *was* his father, and by taking care of the land, he was making up for lost time with his father. He was making amends.

But there was nothing to make amends for because Jimmy hadn't turned his back. He'd simply been pursuing his dream. The way his dad had wanted him to.

"Stop and smell the fresh air along the way," his mother went on. "Have some fun. Meet a good woman and fall in love."

Jimmy couldn't help himself. He thought of Deb. How sexy she'd looked warming up his saddle. How soft and sweet and rumpled when she'd been sound asleep in his bed. How angry when she'd drenched him in the crowded parking lot at the car wash. How vulnerable when she'd talked about her father. How scared when she'd run out on him that morning.

He slipped an arm around his mother and pulled her close for a hug. "I think I've got that last one covered."

I LOVE YOU.

The words echoed through Deb's head throughout the morning, taunting her as she tried to concentrate on the current week's issue. She had to get it out on time and get her life back on track and forget all about Jimmy and the fact that he loved her.

Just where did he get off loving her? He wasn't supposed to love her, and she certainly wasn't supposed to love him.

No matter how out of control he'd been that morning, or how he'd sat up with her all night and helped her fix Annie's dress, or how he'd handed her a tissue without a grin or a smart remark about her crying at the wedding, or how he'd held her and listened to her talk about her father.

Her heart pounded double-time and tears burned the backs of her eyes as she tried to concentrate on her computer keyboard and this week's Fun Girl Fact. She needed something fresh and now and very hip.

Win his heart with fresh-baked tarts!

Heart? This wasn't about winning Jimmy's heart. Not to mention, no true fun girl would be caught dead baking a tart. They stopped by the local deli—or in Inspiration, the House of Pies out on Route 45—for all baked items. No, this was definitely not a fun girl fact and Deb had no desire to win Jimmy's anything, and certainly not with something as tame and domestic as tarts, even if he had expressed a certain fondness for apple-flavored ones.

Boost his ego with banana cream pie!

She thought of Jimmy at the pie festival, his eyes gleaming as he sank his teeth into a slice. No way.

Light his fire with lemon meringue!

Pump him up with peach cobbler!

Seduce his senses with strawberry—

Stop. What was it with all the different pies? She had to steer clear of Jimmy and pies and Jimmy and...

Forget him. Forget that he loves you, and forget that you love him.

She couldn't. She wouldn't.

She stared at the mock-up of tomorrow's edition sprawled across her desk, her gaze snagging on the empty space where her interview with the Mayor should have been. Just this morning, she'd chucked a breakfast question-and-answer session about the town's new parking policy because she'd been too shaken up by Jimmy's declaration to do anything more than rush home and down an entire pot of caffeine.

Because she cared about him. Because she *loved* him.

Denial rushed through her. No, she didn't *love* love him. She was close.... Dangerously close. That's why she couldn't even write a decent Fun Girl Fact anymore. But she wasn't falling all the way, not head over heels, body, heart and soul, in love with Jimmy Mission. Sure, it sounded like a good idea, but once he slid the ring on her finger, he might as well slip the noose over her neck. That would be it. The end of her hard-won freedom. The end of *her*.

No. She'd come too far, struggled too hard. She wouldn't do something as self-destructive as fall in love. Not now. Not ever.

No matter how much she suddenly wanted to.

"WHAT DO YOU MEAN you can't see me?" Jimmy demanded when he stomped into the newspaper office later that afternoon, after a very heated phone conversation. He'd called to ask for a date, no doubt to discuss the bomb he'd dropped that morning. Of course, she'd turned him down.

And turned him down again when he'd called back the second time.

And the third time.

Now here was Jimmy himself, standing in front of her desk wearing a black T-shirt that read Born To Build and faded jeans and an intense look that made her pulse leap.

"Let me rephrase that, I don't *want* to see you." There. She'd said it, despite that she was inhaling the all-too-familiar and terribly sexy scent of warm male and leather and him. Her nostrils flared and her lungs filled, and Deb damned herself for being so weak.

She wasn't weak. She was holding her own, keeping up her defenses, and getting rid of him. Fast. Before Paige or Wally or Dolores came back from lunch and, more importantly, before she gave in to the hunger inside her and kissed him until her toes curled.

"We need to talk—"

"—about this morning," she blurted, "I understand completely. You were worked up and so was I and you didn't mean to say what you said."

"I meant exactly—"

"Oh, God, I'm late!" she screeched, jumping from her chair and moving around the desk to put several feet of wood between them. "Look, you just run along and don't worry that I'm making more out of it than you meant." She gestured wildly toward the door. "And don't worry about forgetting the condom because I'm on the pill."

"I wasn't—"

"We all get a little crazed in the heat of the moment. Chemistry is a powerful thing. People mistake lust for love all the time. Just look at the divorce rate. Lust," she rushed on before he could say anything to shake her determination. "This morning was just a bad case of lust, but now it's sated and—"

"Is it?" he cut in, his gaze deep and searching, as if

he struggled to see everything she was trying so hard
to hide.

"Yes," she declared with as much bravado as she
could muster considering he smelled so good and she
had this insane urge to press her head to his chest just
to hear if his heart was beating as fast as hers. "It's definitely sated."

He eyed her for a long, breathless moment, and she
knew he was going to argue with her. That, or throw
her over his shoulder and tote her back to his cabin
and make love to her over and over until she developed such a craving for him that she couldn't keep
from loving him. And damned if a small part of her
didn't want him to do just that. To take the decision
out of her hands so that she didn't have to think, to
worry, to be afraid of what she felt for him.

What she *almost* felt, she reminded herself. She
wasn't there yet. She wasn't *in* love. She *wasn't.*

As if he sensed the turmoil inside her, his fierce expression eased into his usual charming grin that
never failed to put her nerves on edge.

Oddly enough, it didn't aggravate her. It made her
wary. She couldn't help but get the feeling that rather
than acquiescing, Jimmy Mission had simply
changed tactics.

"Good," he finally drawled, walking around to
perch on the corner of her desk and fold his arms. "If
you're no longer in lust with me, then I don't have to
worry about you jumping my bones while we walk
over to the meeting." At her blank look, he added,
"The town council meeting. You're going and I'm going. We might as well walk together."

"No." She shook her head. "I can't." She moved
back to the other side of the desk.

"So you're not going?"

"I am, but I..." She scrambled for a plausible excuse. "I—I have to stop off at Dolores's along the way. Yeah," she nodded, "I have to stop off and pick up notes from her for her column. And then there's this," she held up a chewed nail courtesy of her frazzled nerves. "I—I have to go by the nail shop for a quickie."

His smile was pure sin and her heart double-thumped. "That sounds interesting."

"A quickie *nail fix*," she qualified. "So I can't possibly walk over with you. And to be honest, I really don't think it's a good idea. I mean, our time together is over. Business concluded. You really should get on with your life, and I'm already zooming right ahead with mine." She made a big show of gathering her notepad and her microrecorder, as if her thoughts were on her work and not the man standing so close to her she could feel the heat of his body.

"You're stubborn, you know that?"

"That's confident, not stubborn. I just know what I want, that's all."

"That's what I'm counting on." He winked before turning toward the door. "I'll see you at the meeting, Slick."

"Not if I see you first," she murmured to herself as he disappeared down the stairwell.

It was all a matter of keeping her distance. Logically, she knew that.

It was the illogical urge to run after him and throw herself into his arms that made her nervous, and all the more determined *not* to love Jimmy Mission.

SHE LOVED HIM.

With any other woman, Jimmy might have had his

doubts. After all, she'd ditched him that morning and practically thrown him out of her office tonight. Sure-fire signs of rejection.

But this was Deb, and she was a far cry from any woman he'd ever known. So different from the hand-ful of women clustered not two feet away in the crowded courtroom where the town council meeting was already underway. All giggling and laughing and casting shy but interested glances his way rather than paying attention to the mayor, who was deep into a proposal for a town project to help the Blakes who'd lost their house to a recent brushfire.

Deb didn't giggle and there was nothing even re-motely shy about her. She was bold and sassy and sexy as hell, and she was scared.

Business concluded, she'd said. He might have be-lieved her, except that he'd seen the wariness in her eyes tonight, heard the desperation in her voice. There'd been none of the cool confidence of a woman completely uninvolved, none of the nonchalance of someone ready to turn her back and walk away be-cause she didn't feel anything for him.

"And round up a crew of volunteers and have our-selves an old-fashioned house-raising. Of course, we'll have to have people with know-how to oversee the construction...."

Yep, she loved him all right, and so Jimmy had backed off when he'd wanted nothing more than to pull her close. He didn't want her afraid of him, of *them*.

He glanced across the crowded courtroom to where she stood near the back entrance. The *back*, when Deb always had a front row seat, eager to challenge the mayor's proposed policies, to question and annoy and work the old guy into a frenzy the way she did every other politician in town.

Not tonight. She'd scanned the sea of faces when she'd walked in, zeroed in on Jimmy for an eighth of a second, and then backed up into the nearest corner, obviously intent on keeping away from him.

"I'll handle the construction," Jimmy called out, drawing every eye, including Deb's. He watched the surprise flash in her expression, then the pleasure, before it disappeared in the same wariness he'd glimpsed earlier.

"Jimmy isn't a crew boss," one of his neighbors piped in. "If you're talking cattle, he's your man. But Cecil over at Cecil's Nail and Hammer could do a better job building a house."

"Except Cecil isn't here tonight, and he isn't volunteering," Jimmy said. "And I am." Because he liked to make things. Because it made him happy.

"Jimmy knows what he's doing." The familiar voice came from the back of the room and sent a burst of warmth through him. His gaze swiveled toward Deb. "He knows everything there is to know about building houses." Her gaze locked with his. "He's the best man for the job."

It took every ounce of control he had not to cross the room and pull her into his arms—a bold, possessive move that would have sent her running for sure, despite her show of support, and Jimmy wasn't about to frighten her off again.

"Then that settles it." The mayor slamming his gavel on the table. "Jimmy's in charge of the house-raising."

She smiled for a brief, dazzling second, before turning her attention back to the notebook in her hand, as if she'd taken a few steps toward him, and she was anxious to retreat.

She had to come to terms with her feelings in her own time, and so he decided then and there that he wasn't going to press or push.

Not too much, that is.

After all, he couldn't just sit quietly by until his stubborn woman came to her senses. That would take too long and Jimmy had never been a patient man when it came to something he wanted, and he really wanted Deb Strickland.

And she wanted him back. She just needed a little help admitting it.

13

"THERE'S A WORD for this, you know," Deb said nearly a week after Jimmy's declaration, when she opened her front door to find him standing on her porch. Again.

The devil danced in his eyes as he grinned. "Courting?"

She ignored the thumping of her heart and glared. "Harrassment. You've shown up every night this week."

As if his presence, so tall and sexy and determined, weren't bad enough, he'd come bearing gifts. Monday he'd shown up with a dozen red roses. Tuesday, he'd brought her a box of chocolates. Wednesday, a bottle of her favorite wine. Thursday, a gift certificate for a year's worth of free manicures. And today, a tuxedo.

She did a double take, her gaze zeroing in on the garment bag draped over his arm. "While I really appreciate the thought, I don't think I'll get much use out of that."

"The tux is for me. This is for you." He handed her a clear florist's box with a wrist corsage nestled inside.

"What for?"

"It's a fancy dress-up affair, so I figured you'd be

wearing a formal. And corsages are appropriate for formals."

"What are you talking about?"

"We have a date."

"We don't—"

"The awards ceremony." He glanced at his watch. "You'd better grab whatever you want to change into. We need to get on the road. Austin is two hours away."

"I told you before, I'm not going."

"You're going."

"I am not."

"Why?"

"Because... I've got a few columns to finish up before tomorrow's deadline and I've already changed into my sweats and my hair's a mess and I...I just can't," she finished when she'd run out of excuses. "Not that I have to explain any of this to you. It's none of your business. I'm not going, end of story."

He stared at her for a long moment, a knowing look in his eyes, as if he saw all her fears and understood them. "You can't run forever," he finally said.

"I'm not running." She met his steady green stare. "I'm right here, nice and settled and enjoying my life. And I'll be enjoying it even more once you leave and let me get back to work."

"Forget running. You already ran and now you're hiding."

"I'm doing no such thing."

"You sure as hell are, Slick." His voice softened. "I know because I've been hiding myself since my dad died. I ran here and buried myself in the ranch, desperate to ignore the life I'd left behind for fear that if I saw what I was missing, I'd be tempted to go back.

You're afraid to see your father, afraid to go back to being that same scared little girl you were when you were living at home."

"I am not."

"You're afraid that your walking away was a fluke and if you see him again, it'll prove that. You're afraid you won't have the courage to stand up to him again."

"I..." the *am not* caught in the sudden tightening of her throat. "I can't go back." She fought against a wave of tears. "I don't want to go back."

Strong, warm fingers cupped her chin and tilted her gaze up to meet his. "This isn't about admitting defeat, baby. It's just an awards dinner. Nothing more if you don't let it be. If you stop hiding and just face it head on."

He was right. She knew that, and as much as she wanted to shut the door in his face because the last thing she needed was a few hours of close contact with Jimmy Mission, she couldn't. A small part of her wanted to go. She'd worked hard for this nomination, and she wanted to enjoy every moment.

Almost as much as she wanted the next few hours with him, sitting side by side, smelling him, feeling him, knowing that he was right there. That's what she'd missed most of all over the past week. More than the touching and the kissing and the heat. She missed the companionship.

"Besides," Jimmy went on, a determined light flaring in his green eyes. "I'm not taking no for an answer."

A grin tugged at her lips. "Is that so?"

"You either come quietly or I'm going to pick you up and tote you to the truck myself."

She was tempted to call his bluff, just to feel his hands on her body one more time. One last time.

She forced the thought aside and gave him a stern look. "Okay, but this isn't a date. That means no funny business."

He arched an eyebrow, his sensual mouth hinting at a grin. "Define what you mean by funny?"

"I mean it, Jimmy. No funny business. No *thinking* about any funny business." He didn't look convinced, so she added, "You stay on your side of the truck and I stay on mine. Tonight we're just two friends accompanying one another to a boring awards ceremony."

His grin widened. "Whatever you say, Slick."

"Promise me." Her heart pounded for several long seconds as she held his gaze. "Please," she finally added.

As if he sensed her desperation, his expression faded and he nodded. "Just friends."

"THIS IS MY FRIEND, Jimmy Mission." Deb introduced Jimmy for the hundredth time to one of her newspaper colleagues during the reception immediately following the ceremony. She cradled her award, her fingers stroking the smooth metal as she smiled and talked and basked in the warm glow of victory.

The evening had been a huge success, all the more memorable because Jimmy had been right beside her, smiling and cheering and sharing in her happiness when the *In Touch* had won Best Weekly.

Happy. Yes, she was definitely happy—especially because the after-ceremony reception was drawing to a close and she'd yet to run into her father. His plane had been delayed. That's what her youngest brother,

Bart, had told her when he'd sought her out to say hello.

"We've missed you, kiddo. When are you coming home?"

She'd held up her award and said, "Inspiration's my home," all the while marveling at how easy the words came, not only the first time, but the next three as she greeted the rest of her brothers and answered the very same question again and again and again.

But those were her brothers whom she still talked to on occasion. They'd shared sporadic phone calls and letters over the years. It was her father who she'd cut herself off from completely. Her father that posed the biggest threat.

One she wasn't going to have to face tonight because he wasn't going to show—

"Deborah Elizabeth." The deep, familiar voice sounded directly behind her and she turned.

"Daddy," she breathed, staring into blue eyes so like her own and a stern expression that never failed to make her stomach tangle into knots.

In a heartbeat, it was as if six years had never passed and she was the same Deborah Elizabeth who'd run from his office that night so long ago. Fear bolted through her and she came close to rushing the other way, but then she felt the warm press of Jimmy's hand at her waist and, just like that, her fear slipped away. He was here and he was right. She had to face this.

"You're looking well," her father told her.

"So are you."

"And doing well, too," he went on, indicating her award. "Congratulations. You made quite a good showing."

"Thanks." She motioned to the six awards sitting on his reserved table several feet away. "You didn't do so bad yourself."

He pursed his lips and shook his head, a gesture she remembered all too well. "We were up for six awards when it should have been seven. It would have been if Robert had sent Carmichael from the Houston office to cover that terrorist attack in Milan instead of Randolph out of Amarillo. The man's a slacker and your brother knew it, but he completely disregarded my advice and took it upon himself..."

As she stood there and listened to him rant about her oldest brother's shortcomings, Deb realized that while she had, indeed, changed over the past six years, her father hadn't. Nothing was ever good enough for him. It never had been and, after seventy-two years, it probably never would be.

Once upon a time that fact had bothered her because she wanted to be the perfect daughter, to win the affection of a man whose only passion had been his work. But as she stood there, Jimmy warm and solid next to her, she realized that it no longer mattered if her father approved of her. She approved of herself.

She was a grown woman now.

Jimmy's woman.

The notion echoed through her head later that evening as she stood on her doorstep, award in hand, and stared at the man who'd walked her up to her front door.

She wasn't *his* woman. She was her own woman. Strong. Confident. *Free.*

"Thanks for tonight." She stuck out her hand to shake his, desperate to keep the distance between them and end the evening before she surrendered to the push-pull of emotion inside her and threw herself into his arms. "I wouldn't have gone if it hadn't been for you and I want you to know that I really appreciate everything...."

He stared at her, into her. "I don't want your thanks."

Her hand fell away. "Please, Jimmy. Don't—"

"I want *you*."

"No, you don't. You want marriage and babies and forever, and I don't." She shook her head and blinked against the burning tears. "I *don't*."

And then she turned and walked away from him, because after six years of clinging to her freedom, Deb didn't know if she had the strength or the courage to let go.

Not that she wanted to. She was happy just the way she was.

Wasn't she?

SHE *WAS* HAPPY, dammit.

That's what she told herself over the next few weeks as she focused on her newspaper and tried to forget Jimmy and the way he'd made love to her so furiously that last time. The way he'd tried his best to woo her over the following days. The way he'd stayed close during the reception, as if she might need him. The way he'd been right there beside her when she had needed him. The way he'd said, *I want you.*

Distance, she told herself. Out of sight, out of mind.

The thing was, Jimmy wasn't exactly cooperative at first. He'd quickly reverted back to his old annoying habits—showing up at various charity dinners and parking in her spot and generally making a sexy, charming nuisance of himself, while she did her best to avoid him. She stayed away from BJ's and the diner and any other place she could possibly run into him and sent Wally and Paige to cover any events that he might happen to attend.

He'd finally gotten the message. She hadn't seen him at all over the past two weeks. He'd obviously pushed aside his feelings and let her go. While the notion made her chest ache for some ridiculous reason she couldn't, wouldn't name, she knew it was for the best. He had to get on with his life, just as she was getting on with hers.

She'd even heard that he and Sarah had gone out on another date. For all she knew, they were taking the first step down the road to matrimony.

She quickly turned her attention back to the article on her desk, a full page dedicated to the kind citizens of Inspiration and their joint effort to build a new house for the Blakes.

Her gaze went to the picture of Jimmy, a tool belt around his waist, his chest bare and sweaty, muscles bunched as he slid a sander across a two-by-four. He sure made one sexy crew boss, and obviously a very capable one. They'd finished the house in record time, despite the storm system that had pushed through central Texas just last week, giving the land some much needed relief from the sweltering weather.

"What do you think of this?" Paige cleared her throat. "Sizzle him with sirloin."

"I think you need to keep working on it." Deb had handed over the Fun Girl Facts column to Paige because, as much as she tried, she didn't feel very fun anymore.

More like sad. Lonely. Miserable.

"I'm outa here." Wally's voice drew her from the depressing thoughts. He topped the stairs from the basement and thrust an empty container of newsprint in the trash. "Cripes," he said as he wiped his hands and glanced at the wall clock. "I'm late."

"For what?"

"I'm covering a wedding," he said, snatching up his camera and pad.

Deb glanced at her list of assignments. "Since when?"

"Since this morning. Pastor Marley called this morning. It's a last-minute thing. See ya."

"But who..." Her words trailed off as the door rocked shut behind him. "Who's getting married?" she asked Paige.

"Beats me."

She glanced at a nearby desk. "Where is Delores when I really need her?"

"Over at the beauty parlor finding out when Donna Simpson is having her next boob job done."

"I haven't heard anything about a wedding." Deb thumbed through the list of upcoming events on her desk. "Who is it?"

"All I know," Paige went on, "is that it's not me. Not now. Not ever again. I'm learning from my mistakes."

"Marriage isn't a mistake. You just hooked up with the wrong man." Was that her own voice taking up for the sacred state of matrimony? "Just because you had one bad go-round, doesn't mean things can't work out the next time." Uh, oh. It *was* her.

"The way things worked out for you and Jimmy?" Paige asked as if reading her thoughts.

"There is no me and Jimmy." Deb stood and gave her most intimidating glare, a look that usually sent shy, timid Paige running for cover.

The young woman had obviously been around Wally a little too long, because she didn't so much as flinch, let alone shudder in fear. She pushed her glasses back up her nose and eyed Deb. "My point exactly. You and Jimmy didn't work out."

"Because there isn't, nor was there ever, a me and Jimmy. We've never been involved." Deb walked to the window in time to see Wally spring across the street and toward the church. A small crowd gathered outside, everyone dressed in their Sunday best, and pure longing shot through her.

Because Deb, despite her freedom-loving claim to fame, wanted her own happily ever after like everybody else. She wanted to waltz down the aisle and drink champagne and feed cake to the man she loved and keep his house and have his babies—albeit with some tasteful designer shoes rather than the proverbial bare feet.

She wanted Jimmy Mission.

And he wanted someone else. The ideal ranch wife.

Just the way her father had wanted the ideal daughter. Someone conservative and obedient and all of the other things that Deb had tried—and failed—to be. That's why she'd run from her feelings for Jimmy. Why she was still running.

She didn't fear losing her freedom half as much as she feared not being what Jimmy wanted in a woman, not being good enough—for the second time in her life.

"The whole town knows he has a thing for you," Paige said.

I love you, he'd said. And maybe he did, but maybe he would wake up one day and realize that he'd made a mistake by loving her. That they had nothing in common, and while love might be enough to bring people together, compatibility kept them together.

"And you have a thing for him," Paige went on. "You love him."

Tears burned the backs of Deb's eyes. "Sometimes that isn't enough," she said, more for herself than Paige. Because sometimes it *wasn't* enough. She'd loved her father, but it hadn't made him return those feelings or accept her for who she was, or even like her. "Sometimes people are just too different."

"Amen to that. Woodrow and I were, and have always been, like night and day, thank the ever-lovin' Lord."

"Love is fine for fairy tales, but we're talking real life," Deb went on.

"Cold, harsh reality," Paige agreed. "Way different."

"I mean, what do I know about ranching?" She shook her head and watched more guests file inside the church. "I'm a city girl in a small town and he's a country boy. We're on opposite sides of the universe." Despite that Jimmy had a particular fondness for chocolate body paint and he looked really great in a black tie and tails—

The thought scrambled to a halt as she did a double take and watched him climb out of his Bronco and cross the street to the church. He paused to shake hands with some of the guests before disappearing inside. Her stomach flipped as the truth hit her.

Jimmy. A church. Black tie and tails.

No!

Panic bolted through her and she was out the door and running before she could stop herself. She took the stairs two at a time and rushed across the street. Jimmy was about to get married and...

She burst through the doors. "Stop!"

A dozen heads swiveled toward her, but she saw only one.

"You can't do this," she blurted as her frightened gaze collided with his, where he stood at the front of the church. "Please. You can't. Not yet." She paused to drink in a frantic breath. "Not until you hear what I have to say. I love you," she rushed on before she lost her courage. "I always have, I just didn't want to tell you because I was afraid you wouldn't love me back because I don't wear Wranglers and I can't wrestle steers or rope a calf or ride a horse or sing even one verse to 'Rawhide'—"

"Slick."

"—and I know that it's important for you to have someone you can share your life with. Someone who likes the same things that you do. And I don't. I mean, I do like some things. I think the cabin's beautiful and the house-raising was a huge success and I could watch you sand wood till the cows come home, but I also like wearing silk skirts and high heels and listening to Ricky Martin and—"

"*Slick!*"

Her frantic thoughts collided to a stop. "What?"

"I haven't wrestled a steer since I was fourteen years old." He stepped toward her. "And I don't sing, period."

"You wear Wranglers," she pointed out.

"Yeah, but I've got a particular fondness for a certain woman in silk skirts and high heels." He reached her then, stopping just a fraction away. "*You*. I've got a major fondness for you, Slick."

"Then don't do this."

"I have to."

The words tightened a vise around her heart and tears burned her eyes. "You can't. *I* want to marry you."

He arched an eyebrow at her. "Is that a proposal?"

"Yes. So don't do this. Don't marry..." She blinked frantically, her gaze darting around looking for Sarah Cook, drinking in the surrounding faces. The pastor. The pastor's wife. His mother. His housekeeper. The head of the ladies auxilliary... "Where is she?"

"I'm afraid he's not the one getting married. It's me." Earline Mission's hand slid into the air and, for the first time, Deb noted the cluster of wild flowers in her hand and a smiling Red Bailey, also in a black tie and tails, standing next to her. "Jimmy's here to give the bride away."

Her gaze swiveled back to Jimmy as realization hit. "You mean I rushed over here and made a fool of myself for nothing?"

"You rushed over here and made a fool of yourself because you love me and I love you. I do, you know. I have since the first moment I saw you sitting in that kissing booth." His grin faded and a serious light gleamed in his eyes. She saw the sincerity in his gaze, felt it in her heart, and she *knew*. She gave in to the longing inside and threw herself into his embrace. Strong arms wrapped around her and held her tight.

"I love you so much," he murmured into her hair. "I love everything about you. I love the clothes you wear and the way you look curled up in my bed and the way your eyes glitter when you're mad. *Everything*."

She pulled back and stared up at him, tears streaming down her face, happiness overflowing her heart. "You forgot Ricky Martin."

He winked. "Actually, I left him out on purpose. While you put up a mighty convincing argument on his behalf—" his eyes twinkled and she knew he was remembering the striptease she'd done for him at the *In Touch* office "—I'm still a big Strait fan."

"Well—" she fingered his collar, a smile playing at her own lips "—I'm not too crazy about George, but I could be persuaded to listen to a Tim McGraw song or two on occasion, in the name of compromise."

And that was it in a nutshell. It wasn't about changing who she was and giving up her sense of self to please Jimmy. It was all about compromise, about two people giving *and* taking.

"Are we going to have a wedding or not?" Red's voice drew their attention and Deb turned to see the impatient look on the older man's face.

"We're going to have a wedding, all right," Jimmy said, his arm tightening around Deb's waist as he gazed down at her. "We're going to have it all. A future filled with love and happiness and lots of kids."

Warmth coursed through her and she smiled. "Don't forget the chocolate body paint," she whispered.

He grinned and drew her close. "A lifetime's worth of chocolate body paint, Slick." And then he kissed her.

_____ Epilogue _____

Two months later...

"CONGRATULATIONS, dear!" The greeting came from one of Earline Mission's fellow church auxilliary members, all thirty-six of whom had turned out to see Inspiration's reputed bad girl finally tie the knot and make a respectable woman of herself.

The site of the auspicious occasion was the Mission Ranch, where they'd erected a huge tent that covered nearly two acres of pastureland. Banquet tables overflowed with everything from barbecue to petit fours—a mingling of city gal meets country boy—while a country-and-western band kept the large dance floor filled with two-stepping guests.

Deb had been busy posing for wedding photographs up until a few minutes ago when the photographer had declared the session over and granted her freedom. Short-lived freedom, of course.

She'd turned and found herself engulfed in a cloud of lilac perfume and Aqua Net.

"Such a lovely wedding, dear."

"And you made such a beautiful bride."

"And Jimmy in his tux is nothing short of a little piece of heaven."

"Why, I bet you two will give Earline and Red the most beautiful grandchildren!"

Deb barely resisted the urge to blurt out, "We'll

find out in about eight months." She wasn't sure, but she had a strong feeling.

Of course, she wouldn't have said anything to the town gossips even if she'd had proof. She didn't give a fig about her own reputation; in fact, she rather liked shocking everyone once in a while. But this wasn't wearing a low-cut blouse to the Bingo hall. This was a child. Deb had never been much for babies, but the notion of having a baby, Jimmy's baby, sent a thrill through her, along with a surge of protectiveness. She wouldn't subject her child to any gossip. Not to mention, she wanted to be the first to tell Jimmy when the time came.

As if the thought had conjured him up, he appeared next to her looking every bit a little piece of heaven right here on earth. Her own private heaven.

"You beautiful ladies don't mind if I dance with my wife, do you?" He smiled and flirted and passed out compliments until he had all of the ladies practically swooning at his feet.

"I still can't figure out how you do that," she said as he led her onto the dance floor and swung her into his arms.

He pulled her closer, rocked his pelvis against hers in a subtle but unmistakable motion, and gave her his infamous grin. "It's all in the hips, Slick. All in the hips."

"Now where have I heard that before?"

"A great woman told me that once before she stripped off her clothes and did unspeakable things to my body."

"Unspeakable, huh?"

"Unspeakable and wicked and shameful, and I

loved every minute." He winked. "That's why I married her."

She smiled, slid her arms around his neck and gave herself up to the wonderful feel of her husband's arms surrounding her, his love filling her up, completing her.

She relished the feeling for the next few moments, until the song ended and they exited the dance floor, and returned to the chaotic reality of a big wedding. It was frenzied and frustrating and all of the things Deb had ever imagined when it came to weddings, and she loved every minute of it, especially since she had her family here with her to share the occasion.

Her brothers and their wives had attended, along with her father who'd done his duty and walked her down the aisle. He hadn't shed a tear or looked even the least bit misty-eyed, but he *had* come and, more importantly, he hadn't voiced a complaint or said one derogatory word to her about her dress or Jimmy or her job.

It was definitely the best day of her life.

"The woman is ruining my life," Wally declared, rushing up to Deb and Jimmy just as they finished cutting the cake.

The woman referred to Paige who stood across the room, a video camera in hand. A new and improved Paige. Not only had she started journalism courses at a nearby community college, but she'd added a few extras like Makeup 101 and Dress for Success and a videography class to her schedule. Gone were the glasses and baggy T-shirts and overalls. She wore contacts now and a simple yet stylish flower-print dress as she practiced her newly learned expertise with Deb's video camera.

"Do you know what these are?" He held up a pair of fuzzy pink handcuffs. "Better yet, do you know where I got them? Do you believe Millie Vernon gave them to me about five seconds ago? They're identical to the ones that Cheryl Plummer handed me at the ceremony and the ones Anita Miller left on the front seat of my car *during* the ceremony." He shook his head. "Why me?"

Paige had inherited the Fun Girl Fact column, along with a few more of Deb's duties—thereby allowing her to do a little sewing on the side. Meanwhile Wally had inherited Jimmy's title as the town's most eligible bachelor, thanks to Paige's recent column on the appeal of the strong, sensitive, studious man.

Most of the single guys in town were ranchers or blue-collar workers, with the exception of Wally, who wore glasses and loafers, read Keats and had just received his bachelor's in journalism. While he wasn't exactly a walking mass of muscles—he looked more like Popeye than Brutus—he hit two out of three which made him a hot commodity.

"And this is nothing," he went on. "Last week I went home to find my bathtub full of pink lemonade. 'Lure him with lemonade.' Have you ever heard anything so corny?"

"Give her a break." Deb licked frosting from her fingertip. "She's still learning. I'd say the handcuffs are definitely a step in the right direction."

Jimmy handed Wally a piece of cake and clapped him on the back. "I feel for you, man. It's a tough job, but somebody has to give the single women in town some hope." His gaze met Deb's and he winked. "I've got my hands full with the married ones."

"And a new business," Deb added.

While Jimmy wouldn't even think of selling the Mission Ranch—it was his home, after all—his heart wasn't in it. He was still in charge, but Wayne, his foreman, saw to the daily running of the place while Jimmy pursued his own dream—Mission Construction. The company had just been hired to build a new courthouse to replace the old one next to the town hall, a feat Deb attributed to the full-page ads she'd been running in the *In Touch* over the past few months.

"So who's minding the ranch while you two set up house at the cabin?" Wally asked.

"Wayne, for now." Jimmy's gaze slid past the reporter to the man standing a few feet away at the bar. "Hey, bro! Come on over here," he called out.

The man set his beer aside and started toward them.

Jack Mission was younger than Jimmy by three years, and every bit as tall and as handsome, but in a different way. While Jimmy was the town's golden boy—all blond hair and green eyes and Texas charm—Jack was every bit the bad boy with his long blond hair and liquid gray eyes and a wildness that made women catch their breath. He was the rebel who roared through town, breaking all the rules and a few hearts along the way. He'd arrived just in time for the wedding, much to the surprise and delight of his brother and mother, and had already caused a stir among the single female population of Inspiration—most of whom stood nearby, gossiping and speculating and waiting to see who among them would catch his fancy.

"Wally, here, wants to know who's minding the ranch," Jimmy said when his brother walked up.

Jack shrugged his broad shoulders. "Don't look at me."

"You're family and you're home now." Jimmy eyed him. "You *could* stick around."

"Maybe." A grin curved his handsome face as he turned and eyed the opposite side of the dance floor where Paige Cassidy stood in her flower-print dress, video camera in hand. "For a little while anyway."

---

*Jack's back in town and has seducing
Paige in his game plan. Little does he guess
that Paige has a few plans for him, too...
Don't miss the fireworks in
RESTLESS, the sizzling sequel to
SHAMELESS, available in November 2000.*

It's hot...and it's out of control.
It's a two-alarm...

BLAZE

This summer, we're turning up the heat.
Look for these bold, provocative, ultra-sexy books!

SHAMELESS by Kimberly Raye
July 2000

Deb Strickland has her hands full—keeping her
small-town newspaper in the black and her hands off
hunky Jimmy Mission. The sexy rancher has come
home to settle down—and that's definitely not in
Deb's plans. It looks like a case of unrequited lust—
until Jimmy makes Deb an offer she can't refuse.
An offer that's absolutely *shameless*....

RESTLESS by Kimberly Raye
November 2000

When bad boy Jack Mission returns home to
Inspiration, Texas, he promptly turns prim and proper
Paige Cassidy's life upside down. Divorced from a man
who swore she could do nothing right, Paige is on a
major self-improvement kick. And sexy, *restless* Jack
is just the man to give her a few lessons in love....

Don't miss this daring duo!

HARLEQUIN®
Temptation

HARLEQUIN® *Temptation.*

Buckhorn County, Kentucky, may not have any famous natural wonders, but it *does* have the unbeatable Buckhorn Brothers. Doctor, sheriff, heartthrob and vet—all different, all irresistible, all larger than life.

There isn't a woman in town who isn't in awe of at least one of them.

But somehow, they've managed to hang on to their bachelor status. Until now...

Lori Foster presents:

Sawyer
#786, On Sale June 2000

Morgan
#790, On Sale July 2000

Gabe
#794, On Sale August 2000

Jordan
#798, On Sale September 2000

The BUCKHORN BROTHERS

All gorgeous, all sexy, all single.
What a family!

Visit us at www.eHarlequin.com   HT4BROS

HARLEQUIN

Duets™

*Pick up a Harlequin Duets™
from August–October 2000
and receive $1.00 off the
original cover price.* *

*Experience the "lighter side of love"
in a Harlequin Duets™.
This unbeatable value just became
irresistible with our special introductory
price of $4.99 U.S./$5.99 CAN. for
2 Brand-New, Full-Length
Romantic Comedies.*

COMING NEXT MONTH

CNM0700